For Team 10
Nerve to Serve
Venezuela, 2001
You guys were awesome!

KATHY WIERENGA BUCHANAN resides in Colorado Springs where she loves spending time with her husband, Sean, and their baby girl. She's on staff at Focus on the Family as a writer and director for the children's radio show, ADVENTURES IN ODYSSEY® and enjoys writing for the Brio Girls® series too. She received her Bachelor's degree from Taylor University and a Master's degree in Biblical Counseling from Colorado Christian University. Kathy is passionate about hiking the mountains, traveling around Italy and, most of all, knowing God intimately and continuing to experience His redemption in her life.

Dear Brio Girl,

If you've ever been on a missions trip, you know they're life-changing experiences. But life-changing doesn't always equal adventure. Getting out of your comfort zone isn't easy. In fact, it can be downright tough. For Jacie, the tough stuff happens when she begins wrestling with questions she can't answer. And Hannah—who's fired up to change South America forever—struggles with unpredictable circumstances in a Latin culture. Follow the Brio gang to Venezuela for a life-changing experience that ensures none of them will return home the same!

And hey! There's a little juxtaposition going on with the Brio gang's missions trip. You see, Brio *really* does *take an annual two-week international missions trip*. So even though you're reading a fantastic story, you have the chance to turn fiction into reality by actually signing up for the trip! Go ahead and download the information packet from our Web site: www.briomag.com. We guarantee that you, too, will return never the same!

Your Friend,

Susie Shellenberger, BRIO Editor
www.briomag.com

BRIO GIRLS®

from Focus on the Family®
and
Tyndale House Publishers, Inc.

brio girls

REAL Faith MEETS REAL Life

Jacie Tyler Solana Becca

Croutons for Breakfast

Created by

LISSA HALLS JOHNSON

WRITTEN BY KATHY WIERENGA BUCHANAN

TYNDALE

Tyndale House Publishers, inc.
Wheaton, Illinois

A Focus on the Family book published by
Tyndale House Publishers, Inc., Wheaton, Illinois 60189; First printing, 2005
Previously published by Bethany House under the same ISBN.

Tyndale's quill logo is a trademark of Tyndale House Publishers, Inc.
BRIO GIRLS is a registered trademark of Focus on the Family.

Cover design by Lookout Design Group, Inc.
Editor: Lissa Halls Johnson
Cover inset and background photos by Lissa Halls Johnson

This story is a work of fiction. With the exception of recognized historical
figures, the characters are the product of the author's imagination. Any
resemblance to any person, living or dead, is coincidental.

Library of Congress Cataloging-in-Publication Data

Wierenga, Kathy.
   Croutons for breakfast / created by Lissa Halls Johnson ; written by Kathy
Wierenga.
       p. cm. — (Brio girls)
   "A Focus on the Family book."
   Summary: Hannah and Jacie both undergo personal transformations as God
reveals Himself to them in new ways on a Brio missions trip to Venezuela.
   ISBN 1-58997-080-2
   [1. Missionaries—Fiction. 2. Christian life—Fiction. 3. Venezuela—
Fiction.] I. Johnson, Lissa Halls, 1955-   II. Title. III. Series.

   PZ7.W63583Cr   2002
[Fic]—dc21   2002153700

Printed in the United States of America

11 10 09 08 07 06 05
9 8 7 6 5 4 3 2 1

chapter

"Make room for the cookies!" Mrs. Connor set the overflowing plate in the middle of the mass of papers.

Tyler rescued a soft, steamy cookie ready to slide off the plate. "Well," he said with a twinkle in his eye, "since you went to all the trouble of making them . . ."

Becca grabbed one too. "I suppose I'll make the sacrifice as well."

Jacie gnawed on the top of her pen, mindlessly twirling one of her springy curls. Her ability to think vanished as she stared at the words in front of her.

Why do you want to go on the Brio Missions Trip?

Why *did* she want to go? She surveyed the table. Hannah, Tyler, and Becca were already two questions ahead of her on their applications. Apparently, they knew their answer.

Jacie used to know. When Tyler galloped into Alyeria—their secret meeting place in a grove of aspen trees—waving a *Brio* magazine and jabbering about how awesome it would be to go on a missions trip together, it seemed like a great idea. Inspired by Hannah's and Becca's enthusiasm, the four had talked about little else. Two weeks in Venezuela with 400 other teenagers—what could be better? It was the ultimate summer adventure. But now it seemed too real. Too soon. Too scary. The application lay in front of her waiting for the right answers.

"Jacie, if you want a cookie, you'd better grab one," Hannah said. Wisps of long, blonde hair escaped from her loosely tied bun, and her clear blue eyes sparkled.

The cookies were already half gone. Jacie bit into the one Becca handed her. It had been a while since she'd had homemade chocolate chip cookies. Jacie's mom didn't have time to bake. She bought Chips Ahoy sometimes, but it wasn't the same—even when Jacie zapped them in the microwave.

Mr. Connor entered the dining room. "How's it going?"

"Delicious," said Tyler through a mouthful of cookie. Jacie noted that his surfer-cut sandy hair was beginning to show the highlights of summer. She sighed.

Mr. Connor leaned in to read over Hannah's shoulder.

"Dad, you're making me nervous," Hannah said, playfully smacking him.

"I'm just making sure you answer question number five thoroughly. I don't think there's enough room there to list all your strengths. Tyler, hand her another sheet of paper."

"Coming right up." He wadded up a piece of paper and tossed it in Hannah's direction. As she grabbed for it, it bounced off her hand and spiraled onto the dining room rug.

"Ability to catch is not one of those strengths," smirked Becca.

Hannah tossed her pen at Becca—and missed by at least a foot.

Jacie smiled at their antics, then returned to the question. "Why did we decide to go on this trip?" she asked.

"Because there are so many people in Venezuela who don't know Christ," said Hannah.

"Because we get to explore a different country and meet a bunch of other kids and do work projects to make people's lives better," Becca said.

"Because there are 20 girls to every guy," said Tyler. "But you probably shouldn't use that as your answer."

"I hope you didn't use that either," said Jacie. She rested her chin on her hands and tapped her latte-colored cheeks. No one else worried about their motives or being accepted to go on the trip. Only she did. Already her mind swirled with concerns about raising support, traveling to a different country, contracting the bubonic plague—

"Just think," Hannah said, glowing. "In a few months we'll be praying with people to receive Christ who have never heard the gospel before. How exciting!"

Oh yeah. Evangelizing. Not Jacie's strongest gift. In fact, the bubonic plague didn't sound nearly as bad as approaching strangers with an open Bible.

But isn't a missions trip all about evangelism?

"Why am I going? I'm not good at these kind of things," she moaned, dropping her head onto the table.

"You're going because you're great with people," said Tyler.

"Because you love others and want to help," added Becca.

"Because you love God and you want to follow His command to go into all the world and spread His salvation message," said Hannah.

No, I don't, Jacie almost said out loud. She thought she loved God, but if she really loved Him, wouldn't she be more eager to share her faith? Wouldn't she be less frightened? Her friends all did it. She could draw or paint her faith, but she couldn't share through spoken words. Those never flowed like a charcoal pencil on her sketchpad.

She figured she'd better write Becca's suggestion. She knew that much was true.

Why do you want to go on the Brio Missions Trip?

Because my mom and I have never had much, I understand what it's like to be poor. I always try to pay attention when others need to feel loved and help them in some way. I know the people we'll be ministering to in Venezuela don't have a lot. And I want to show them God's love and provision like it has been shown to me and my mom. I can't give them much, but I will give them whatever I can to make their lives better.

● ● ●

Hannah played with her pencil, mulling over the final question on her application.

Describe your current relationship with God

The pencil flipped out of her hand, flew across the table, and jabbed Tyler.

"Augh!" He fell to the ground, clutching his shoulder. "I . . . think you . . . killed . . . me."

"Good," said Becca. "There'll be more cookies for the rest of us."

"Hey, wait!" Tyler jumped back into his chair. "Save some for me!"

Hannah grinned at her friends. She never imagined on her first day at Stony Brook High School last September that she'd become so tight with this group. She thanked God every day for helping her find Christian friends so quickly. She found they challenged her in her faith more than she expected.

The doorbell rang.

Hannah's little sister, Rebekah, ran to the door with the six-year-old twins padding behind her.

Hannah picked up another pencil. Telling how she became a Christian was easy—but describing her relationship with God was more of a challenge. Reading her Bible and praying every day were as habitual as brushing her teeth. *But what is God doing in my life right now?*

"It's Solana," called Rebekah, opening the door.

"It's Solana," the twins echoed.

"It's Solana!" The heralding voice made its way into the dining room before the raven-haired speaker appeared. Solana waltzed up to the table, flashing a smile framed in bright red lipstick. "How are the applications going, *mis amigos?*" She slipped smoothly into an empty chair. "My friends. The saints."

"It's going great," said Hannah.

"I'm glad you decided to grace us with your presence," Becca said.

Solana batted her eyelashes. "Well, I went horseback riding this morning, but I thought I might be able to convince Monk Tyler and the rest of you nuns to take a break and go to Copperchinos with me."

"Sounds good to me," said Tyler. "I'm almost done."

"Not me," Jacie said.

Mrs. Connor peeked around the corner. "Hi, Solana. Would you like some cookies? I'm taking a fresh batch out of the oven." Hannah noticed her mom's eyebrows shoot up when she saw Solana's short denim skirt.

"No thanks, Mrs. Connor."

Hannah tried to focus on the application as her friends chatted, but her mind kept wandering back to Solana. On numerous occasions, Hannah had tried to convince Solana of the eternal importance of becoming a Christian. And she knew her other friends had witnessed to her for years before that. *God, it just goes to show how closed off people become when they refuse to open their eyes to the truth. At least in Venezuela, people are hungry for the truth.* She pictured masses of people surrounding her, wide-eyed and silent as Hannah revealed the gospel message to their eager ears and hungry hearts.

Describe your current relationship with God.

My current relationship with God could be characterized by the word "growing." I think God is showing me new ways that He can use me to build His kingdom. He's given me the ability to be outspoken and articulate about my faith. He's given me knowledge about His Word. And He's given me a heart for the lost and a desire to share the truth—and I'm excited to see what He'll do on this missions trip.

chapter 2

I can't believe we're on a plane to Miami!
There's no turning back now. Over the last few
months, there were times when I thought,
"Wow! What could be better? Two weeks with
my best friends in an exotic foreign country!"
At other times I thought, "What could be
worse? I don't like flying, evangelizing, or eating
strange food!" But now, for better or worse,
it's happening.

Even though Mom cried at the security gate,
she kept saying how lucky I am to be going—as
if I haven't heard that enough over the past
few months. She told me again that it will
change my life. She seemed so proud—why?

7

On the other hand, Dad called to say he couldn't understand why I'd go on a missions trip at all. Weren't there better things to do with my summer? Or better places to go? However, he did send me a top-of-the-line camera.

Yesterday, I was so stressed about the trip, I went to the shack to paint. When the brush started to slide across the canvas, I thought it would end up being Caracas or Colorado in the summertime. But instead I painted Dad, just standing there, staring across the San Francisco bay. And me, off to one side, just standing there, staring at him.

Jacie shut her journal, running her finger along the Chinese design on the front. The plane pulled away from the gate, and her stomach shrank into a tighter knot. No matter how many times she'd flown to California to see her dad, she still got queasy at the thought of flying. There was always something to be afraid of. Always.

Initially, the most daunting part of the missions trip was raising the money. She hated asking others for money. Hannah said they were blessing people by allowing them the opportunity to take part in "kingdom work." *That did sound better than "begging for cash,"* Jacie thought.

The plane taxied down the runway. She'd hoped to sit next to one of her friends, but instead, they were scattered. Tyler, a few rows in front of her, was wearing headphones. She couldn't see him, but she knew he was also reading *Guitar Guy* magazine. Hannah was seated across the aisle from him, probably reading her Bible. Earlier, Hannah had chatted with the flight attendant about Venezuela. Becca sat near the back surrounded by a college softball team, no doubt feeling right at home.

"Pretty ring," said the man seated next to Jacie. The large man squeezed into the small airline seat made Jacie think of what the Pillsbury Doughboy might look like stuffed into a Dixie cup.

"Thanks," Jacie smiled. "My dad gave it to me years ago."

"Are you from Miami?" he asked. She could smell pretzels on his breath. Remaining crumbs stuck in the chest hair escaping from his low-buttoned shirt.

"Nope. Just visiting."

The tough-looking older woman on the other side twitched her mouth and began muttering under her breath, "I don't know why they don't allow smoking on flights anymore. They even fine you if they catch you lighting up in the bathroom these days."

"I know," Jacie said. She thought this woman must be the world's oldest biker chick. Her black leather jacket smelled of gasoline and stale smoke.

"I hate flying. Hate it. This thing's gonna crash. I just know it." The plane shuddered and the woman gasped.

"I'm sure we'll be fine." Jacie tried to sound confident in spite of her own similar thoughts. Her stomach lurched as the plane skipped from the runway and ascended.

The fat man continued, "I've lived in Miami for 20 years. I know everyone in that town."

The granny-biker pressed her nose against the window. "Look at those wings wobble. They're going to fall off any minute now."

"The wings always move," Jacie said. "But they won't fall off." She watched the trembling wings out the window. *Are they shaking more than usual?*

"Why would you want to visit Miami in the summer?" the man asked. "Humidity will suffocate you."

"Should have updated my will before I left. Should have taken that no-good nephew of mine out." The woman clasped and unclasped her hands.

Jacie took a deep breath. "I'm going on a missions trip to Venezuela."

"A missions trip? Are you building a church or somethin'?"

"Did you see how young that pilot is? Doubt he could navigate a bicycle, much less a plane." The woman shook her head.

"We're going to be sharing the gospel through drama and work projects." *I sound like the brochure.*

"Oh. Like one of those cults. You pray all the time and stuff?" the Dough Boy asked.

"Do you feel this thing shake? Maybe you should start praying for this plane." Biker Grandma gripped the armrest and nodded toward the wing.

Jacie looked straight ahead. She wouldn't get scared. She wouldn't think about being on an airplane thousands of feet above the ground in nothing but empty air. "I'm not in a cult. I'm a Christian and . . . that's different."

"You people used to come to my door all the time. Telling me I was going to hell and stuff," the man said.

"And they expect that emergency door to save us? What good is an emergency door when it's 30,000 feet in the air?" the woman complained.

The man barely paused. "Once I asked them what was so good about heaven, and they told me it has streets of gold. Seems pretty stupid to me. Asphalt works just fine."

"I'm not worried about getting out of the plane. When this wing falls off, there will be plenty of space to get out. I'm worried about getting safely to the ground," the woman said, oblivious to everything else.

"Told them to get their suits back on their bikes and go bother someone else."

"What good is a seat cushion that floats anyway? Why don't they give you parachutes instead?"

Jacie finally gave up bouncing back and forth to keep up with both conversations. She couldn't get a word in edgewise anyway. And even if she could, she wouldn't know what to say. *If Hannah were sitting here, she'd know what to say. She'd be able to explain Christianity, comfort Biker Grandma, and assure them both that God is in control. Shoot, they'd probably all be singing "Amazing Grace" in three-part harmony if Hannah were in this seat.*

But Hannah wasn't in the seat. Jacie was. And Jacie wasn't good at this kind of thing.

● ● ●

Eventually, Jacie's two seatmates calmed down. Biker Grandma, who introduced herself as Edith, slept peacefully on Jacie's left shoulder. Dough Boy—also known as Craig—snored loudly on her right. Jacie tried to keep her upper body still as she thumbed through the fashion magazine the flight attendant had brought her. Observing her plight, Tyler winked at Jacie as he made his way back to the restroom.

"How precious. That's so you," he smiled. "Everyone loves Jacie."

Jacie smiled back. She didn't know how, but she was a master at getting people's minds off things. Her stories about her friends' antics had reminded Edith of her grandkids, and the row ended up poring over the old woman's photos before she and Craig drifted off.

Jacie tried to find an interesting article. "Highlights You've Gotta Have." "20 Sunny Summer Styles." "Guy Guide: Turn His Eyes Your Way." Nothing new here. She'd seen these "tips" a hundred times before.

● ● ●

"We're now making our final descent into the Miami International Airport," the flight attendant announced over the intercom. "Please make sure your seatbelts are fastened, tray tables up, and your seats are in their upright position."

Jacie shifted—gently, then a little more forcefully—to wake Edith and Craig. Beyond Edith, out the window, Jacie could see the city of Miami spread out like a postcard. Beyond huge buildings and neighborhoods of suburban homes, an expanse of murky marshland stared back. Jacie's breath caught in her throat. This was it. The start of two weeks of work projects, learning a drama, sharing the gospel, traveling around a different country, and meeting hundreds of new people. She had no idea what to expect, only that it was an adventure waiting to happen. *And I don't think I'm ready.*

● ● ●

"Just like I remember. Muggy—a soggy air blanket," Tyler said. Even in the air-conditioned airport, the air felt heavy.

Jacie, Becca, and Tyler shifted impatiently while Hannah talked with the young mother who'd sat next to her on the plane. Jacie noticed guys eyeing Hannah as they passed. Hannah always looked beautiful—even in long khaki culottes and no makeup.

"Well, I'll be praying for you. I hope your mother feels better soon." The woman thanked her and left, toting her whimpering child behind.

"Okay, before we go anywhere, I need to get a picture of you all at the gate." Hannah dug in her carry-on for her camera.

"Why?" asked Tyler.

"Because it's part of our journey!" she said. She deftly arranged her three friends. "Now pretend you're just getting off the plane. Make it real."

Jacie stuck out her tongue.

Tyler pretended to strangle Jacie.

Becca sniffed her armpit.

"Close enough," sighed Hannah.

Click.

"What now?" Becca asked.

"There's supposed to be someone here to meet us," Tyler said. "I thought Mom might come herself, but she's probably swamped today."

As part of the *Brio* staff, Tyler's mom had flown out a few days earlier to set up.

"I think that's probably our guy," Becca pointed to a man, rushing toward them wearing a teal "Nerve to Serve" T-shirt that mirrored their own. The shirts had been mailed a few weeks ago, with a request that they be worn the day the kids arrived.

"Welcome to Miami!" The broad-shouldered man grinned at them, making his eyes crinkle. Jacie liked him immediately. He reminded her of a big teddy bear. "I'm Harold Berkowitz, but most people call me Berk." He glanced at the sheet of paper in his hand. "You must be Tyler." He shook Tyler's hand.

"Yup," Tyler laughed. "But I'm the easy one. Good luck guessing the others."

"No problem." Berk examined each girl's face. "Hannah, Becca, and Jacie." He said, pointing to each.

"How'd you know?" Becca asked.

"Your names fit." Berk shouldered Becca's backpack and held out his hand for Jacie's bag.

"Thanks," Becca said.

"Baggage claim is this way," he said, pointing with his free hand. "Names are important to me, kind of a hobby, I guess. My oldest daughter is named Hannah."

"Really?" Hannah asked.

"Yep." Berk looked back at her. "It means 'full of grace, mercy, and prayer.'"

"That's Hannah all right," Tyler said. "No one prays like she does."

Hannah's cheeks turned pink.

"I thought it might mean blonde goddess," joked Becca.

Hannah's pink cheeks reddened.

Berk shifted to Becca. "And I'm assuming 'Becca' comes from 'Rebecca.'"

"And it means 'the captivator,'" Becca said, raising her chin proudly.

"Like Rebekah captivated Isaac in the Bible," nodded Berk.

"Why, Becca, I suddenly can't keep my eyes off you," Tyler said, walking zombie-like toward Becca.

The group laughed.

"Now, 'Jacie,'" Berk continued. "That's a pretty name, but I have no idea what it means."

"Same here," Jacie said. "Every time I look for my name on personalized mugs and stuff I can never find it."

"We'll have to figure it out," Berk said.

A river of teal shirts suddenly absorbed the small group, swarming around them. Jacie couldn't believe how many "Nerve to Serve" T-shirts there were in the airport. It was reassuring to see all of them— somehow things didn't seem so scary with 400 others beginning the same journey she was. And they were all instantly bonded by a T-shirt.

"So how about my name, Berk?" Tyler asked.

The middle-aged man smirked. "Maker of tiles or bricks, I believe."

"Ooh! That's exciting," Tyler said ruefully. "I was thinking more along the lines of 'big, strong man with cool hair.'"

"We can call you that if you want," Berk said. "Or how about just 'Cool Hair' for short."

"Sounds like a rap star," Becca said.

"Well, I am a musician," Tyler added.

The girls exchanged amused looks. Jacie wouldn't exactly categorize Tyler as a musician, but if tone-deaf and off-key ever became the rage, he'd top the charts.

"What about your name, Berk?" Jacie asked.

"Well, as much as I'm not a huge fan of the name Harold, the meaning is appropriate."

"What is it?" Becca's curiosity peaked.

"Army commander."

"Why is that appropriate? Were you in the military?" Hannah asked.

"Nope. But for the next two weeks I'll be a team leader for you and Jacie."

"We're on your team?" Jacie asked, delighted. Berk's warmth made her feel instantly comfortable.

"Yep. But remember, I'm the army commander." He gave Jacie a mock-stern look. "Mess with me, and you'll be doing push-ups."

Jacie saluted. "Yes, sir."

chapter

Hannah stared out the window of the shuttle van. Miami seemed to be nothing but traffic, highways, and cement. She'd packed her athletic shoes in case there was a park nearby where she and Becca could go running, but it didn't look like that would be happening. And where was the ocean? She kept her face to the window, feeling shy in this group of people she didn't know. Jacie, on the other hand, had already met everyone on the van—including the driver. She also had everyone talking. "Where are you from? Is this your first missions trip? Are you nervous?" Hannah almost laughed at how she and Jacie had swapped places from the plane. Hannah could talk to anyone—as long as they were adults. Jacie could talk to anyone—as long as they were kids.

Hannah exchanged amused glances with Becca and Tyler.

It's funny how we're all comfortable in different situations, she thought. Jacie was best surrounded by people. Becca felt most at home on any athletic court or field. Tyler preferred anywhere he was getting female attention—be it rock climbing or strumming his guitar. And Hannah . . . Hannah liked places she could be open about God and spread her knowledge of Him. She knew she'd shine over the next couple weeks.

The van pulled into a covered driveway and stopped at the hotel entrance. Lush tropical plants grew on each side of the pillared doorways. The group scrambled out of the van, eager for the next part of the adventure—which happened to be hugs from two smiling grandma-types.

"Welcome! Welcome!" the cheerful women called.

Tyler spotted a friend from a previous trip. He pounced on him from behind and the two started wrestling. Becca joined a game of Hacky Sack commencing on the sidewalk. Jacie spoke with two girls from Alaska, her curls bouncing in rhythm with her speech.

Hannah watched, feeling different from her friends. But that didn't really matter. She'd grown accustomed to being "different." She preferred long culottes to cutoffs and classical music over the latest pop star. She'd rather spend her money on photography equipment than makeup or movies. And courtship made more sense than dating. She'd always felt more comfortable in church than in school. And she'd feel more comfortable on a missions trip than hanging out at the mall.

She pulled her camera out of her bag and began snapping candids of the Hacky Sack game. It was easy to hide behind a camera—it made her look occupied when she didn't know what else to do. Plus, she needed some pictures to send in her "thanks for your support" letters when she returned home. That gave her a thought. *I could get pictures of all the people I lead to Christ!* The thought made her smile.

Click. Click.

Through the viewfinder, she saw her friends join the snaking registration line in the lobby.

She put down her camera and slipped into line with Jacie.

"Hannah, meet Phoebe," Jacie said. "She's on our team."

"Hi! It's nice to meet you." Hannah gave Phoebe the once-over. She wouldn't have guessed there'd be someone like this petite girl on a missions trip. She wore a laced-up peasant blouse, camouflage cutoffs, and a red bandana over her short, shaggy hair.

Phoebe tugged at a lock of hair. "Yesterday, I knew I had to go blonde. For the past month I'd sworn by Crazy Cranberry until it became mega-popular. Now Potently Platinum is my color of choice. I like making trends, not being a part of them."

Me too, thought Hannah. *That's why I don't color my hair.*

"I like it," Jacie said.

"You've got to see this hotel. It's nothing like Boston," Phoebe said. "There's a rain forest in the middle of this one. Mega-cool."

Phoebe was right. The jungle atrium they walked through on the way to the elevators was "mega-cool." The entire hotel was cool. Every floor had a balcony that looked down onto the lush indoor park, which had been filled with tropical plants and palm trees, birds, stone walkways, and a giant waterfall flowing into a rippling stream.

Tyler came up behind them. "Ladies, we're not in Colorado anymore."

Becca's face lit up. "We're going to have such a great time!"

Tyler's eyes followed a group of long-legged, giggling girls. "A great time," he repeated.

"Tyler!" The three girls scolded in unison.

"What? I'm not doing anything . . ."

The three girls glared at him.

He put up his hands in defense. "Okay, okay. I'll just go over here and take the stairs to my room since I'm only on the second floor. I'll catch you guys at FUAGNEM."

"Foo-ag-what?" asked Hannah.

"FUAGNEM. Fired Up And Going Nuts Every Minute—it's the worship rally we have every night where we get together and hear Susie speak. It's way fun."

Hannah nodded. "Good. Church every night is good."

Tyler smirked. "Well . . . yeah. Sort of."

"I'll take the stairs with you, Ty," Becca said. "This way I can help those *señoritas* fend you off."

Jacie and Hannah crowded onto a waiting elevator.

"It's weird being here without Solana," Jacie said.

Hannah nodded. Though the fifth member of the close-knit group wasn't a Christian, it felt strange to be together without her—even on a missions trip.

"She hasn't been the same since the whole Ramón incident," Jacie said. "I felt sort of like we were abandoning her when we left."

The elevator bell dinged at the fifth floor and the girls got out, dragging their bags behind them.

"We'll have a lot to tell her when we get back," Hannah said. "Maybe something will finally make her understand how much she needs Christ." She constantly racked her brain trying to figure out something to say—an illustration or the perfect verse—that would make Solana realize the truth of the gospel. "God has to honor our prayers eventually. Like the parable of the widow and the unjust judge . . ."

"I know, you've told us before." Jacie rolled her eyes. "The widow pounded on the judge's door and asked for justice until the judge finally gave it to her." Jacie paused. "I don't think that's really how God is, do you? Not giving in until we ask enough times? Like we could ask 999 times, but until we ask the thousandth time, He won't give in?"

Hannah realized she'd never thought about it that way. She tried to cover her bewilderment. "Well, of course not," she said, while inside, the whole thing really bugged her.

They dropped their bags in front of room 512 and turned to lean over the railing. Masses of teal T-shirts moved about below.

Jacie continued, "For years, I prayed the same thing morning, noon, and night. I thought God would have to answer my prayer eventually."

"What did you ask for?"

Jacie gave a sad smile. "My parents to get back together, get married, and live happily ever after."

"That's a good prayer," Hannah said wistfully.

"Apparently not good enough."

Hannah stared over the railing. In the past she'd tried to share verses that might comfort her friend, but Jacie didn't seem to appreciate it. She tried to remind herself that sometimes, just listening was best, but she found it very hard to be quiet.

"When did you stop asking?" Hannah asked.

"Not until the day Dad married Felicia. Even after they were engaged, I still prayed—harder than ever—that he'd want to come back and be part of our family. But when Felicia walked into that garden ceremony and I saw how he looked at her, I knew he would never come back. I cried through the whole thing."

Hannah nodded. She knew God wanted families to stay together. That was His design. But she also knew Jacie's dad wasn't a Christian. *But if the unbeliever leaves, let him do so . . .*

"C'mon," Jacie said. "We didn't ride on a plane for five hours to talk about me. We can do that in Copper Ridge. Let's go in and get settled."

They opened the hotel room door to a party already in progress. Jacie's contemplative mood seemed to dissipate as she immersed herself in meeting the next new sea of faces. A freckled redhead named April. A tiny, sweet Southerner named Laurilee. An athletic tomboy named Valerie. A spunky African-American girl named Nichole. And six more names that escaped Hannah's brain the moment they were introduced.

"Are we all in here together?" Hannah asked, looking around the small suite.

"I don't think so, girlfriend. Jus' six a' us is in here. The rest of these Team 10 girls is jus' chillin'."

Hannah forced a smile. All she could think was *I hope they don't snore*.

"Y'all, I am so excited I could crawl outta mah skin!" drawled Laurilee.

Dear God, Hannah prayed. *I know I'm supposed to love them. Just help me remember their names for two weeks.*

● ● ●

Hannah stuck close to Jacie as they entered the freezing meeting room for FUAGNEM. Kids shouted to each other and sat cross-legged in groups on the carpeted floor. A Frisbee zipped between two guys. Leaders sat on chairs lining the perimeter of the room. The noise in the room escalated as the groups grew larger. Beach balls flew overhead as fists rose to punch them. Finger rockets shot like blue missiles to knock the beach balls out of orbit. Shrieks rose when the unsuspecting got bonked by a rocket or ball. *Wow*, Hannah thought. *It's like a playroom for teenagers.* Jacie joined right in with the rest of them, laughing her hee-haw donkey laugh—the one that slipped out when she was having too much fun to notice.

"You look lost." Phoebe's face popped in front of Hannah's. She linked her arms through hers and Jacie's. "We're all sitting up front. I am so psyched! The band is setting up, and they look mega-wild!"

Once the music started, Hannah had to admit that although the band was not one she might usually like, they were really good. The roomful of energized teens danced, swayed, and sang along with the music. Hannah looked around, astounded. This wasn't at all what she'd expected the evening worship to be like.

The music stopped and as the teens cheered, hooted, and whistled, a supremely confident Susie Shellenberger strode to the microphone. "And now, without further ado," she announced, "presenting your favorite superhero and mine: Rrrredman!"

People cheered, not knowing what they were cheering for. Suddenly, a tall, but not-so-super, hero appeared on stage covered in red spandex from head to toe. Only his eyes could be seen. He moved stiffly and precisely onto the stage. But when the music started again, he danced like a wild man—floppy arms flailing, body contorting. The moment the music stopped, a subdued Redman wheeled mechanically on one foot and walked stiffly down the stairs and out the side door. The crowd cheered, shouting for more. Hannah looked around, not quite getting it.

She leaned over and whispered into Jacie's ear, "What's the point of Redman?"

"I think the point is there is no point."

"Oh."

Over the next few minutes, Susie paced the stage, sharing how everyone needs to be born into God's kingdom. And those who have been born again, she said, have a reason to celebrate. "So," she continued, "we're going to end this evening with—you got it—a birthday party for you! Let's put some music on and pass out cake. Happy birthday, everyone!"

After a rousing chorus of "Happy Birthday," Tyler and Becca found Hannah and Jacie. "Just like a church service, huh, Hannah?" he said through a mouthful of cake.

"Well, Susie did teach from the Bible, but it was a little different than church." Hannah smiled.

"I could get used to church like this," Jacie said, crumbs clinging to the corner of her mouth.

"Me, too," Becca said.

● ● ●

After FUAGNEM Hannah found a café table hidden behind a palm. She had a few minutes to journal before her first Team 10 meeting. She slipped into the chair and removed her journal from her backpack.

Jesus, tonight it was fun to celebrate my birth into Your family. I'm very excited to be on a trip where many will be accepting You into their lives. I want to do a good job for You. I don't want to be lazy or scared. I want to represent You well, so I've decided to set some goals for myself for the next two weeks.

1. Help my team learn the most effective ways to evangelize non-believers.
2. Be a good Christian example to my teammates. Offer them words of encouragement.
3. Lead 20 people to the Lord. (But I don't want to limit You to that, God. I know You can do so much more!)
4. Pray for a different team member or leader daily.

Hannah read back over the goals. They sounded pretty good. She returned her journal to her backpack and zipped it shut, feeling content. She might not be as popular as Jacie, but God was going to use her gift of evangelism on this trip. She just knew it.

Jacie looked around the motley group. Could she really get to know all these people as friends? Tyler's mom had warned the four Colorado friends that they probably wouldn't all be together. Still, Jacie hoped she'd at least be with Tyler or Becca—but not Hannah. Not that she didn't like Hannah, but in situations like these, when she was likely to feel scared, lost, or needy, Tyler was the one who always helped her face her fears and be brave. He gave her courage. Hannah made her feel small and stupid.

"Yo! Team 10!" Berk shouted through his cupped hands. "Welcome to the Brio Missions Trip!"

"Yo!" the group cheered in response.

"I'm Berk, and this is Melanie," he said, pointing to a motherly-looking, plump woman. She waved, a cheerful smile crinkling her entire face.

As Berk explained the schedule for the next two days in Miami, Jacie looked around. *Will these kids like me? Will I like them?*

"My name is Morgan," said an older Asian girl with manicured nails and thick black hair that fell to the middle of her back. "And something interesting about me is that I was schooled in Europe for three years."

They must have asked us to introduce ourselves. Jacie groaned inwardly. She hated doing things like this. Everyone claimed she was a natural. But she didn't see it. She felt stupid and struggled when it came to thinking up clever things to say.

A blond guy with sparkling brown eyes took his turn. "Hey, everyone! I'm Corey." *Cute smile,* thought Jacie, and she could tell a lot of the other girls agreed. "And I'd like to be a fighter pilot someday."

A perky brunette sat next to him, smiling coyly. "I'm Celia," she said. "And one interesting thing about me is that I'd like to date a fighter pilot someday."

Corey blushed and the rest of the group laughed.

"I'm Lia," said a large-boned girl that Jacie had heard talking up a storm earlier. She twirled her long brown ponytail between her fingers. "And . . . let's see . . . I have 12 toes. I'm allergic to redheads. And these aren't my original limbs."

"Lia . . ." warned Berk.

"Okay, I'm kidding," grinned Lia. "But the true interesting thing is that Berk here," she walked over to the leader and did a Vanna White pose in front of him, "is my dad and he's awesome." She squeezed in next to him on the little bench.

"Thanks, Sweetie." An affectionate father-daughter look passed between them as Berk put his arm around Lia and pulled her in tight. Lia leaned her head against her dad's shoulder.

An ache and a longing took root inside Jacie. She couldn't bear to watch what she couldn't have. Jacie distracted herself by listening to the others introduce themselves. As they did, Jacie felt increasingly out of place. Everyone here was confident, fun, and interesting.

When her turn came, Jacie jumped to her feet. "Hi, my name is

Jacie," she said, offering a quick little wave and a big smile. Everyone smiled back—including Corey, she noticed. "And I guess I'm supposed to come up with something interesting to say." She shrugged with her palms held up for emphasis. She looked up at the sky, her mind racing. Suddenly, the words burst out of her before she could stop them. "I can walk on my hands and gargle at the same time." She bit her lip. *Stupid, but true*.

"Awesome!" Corey said. "You've got to show us sometime."

That released Jacie's full smile. "Of course. Show times are at five and nine. Bring an umbrella. The gargling can get out of hand."

Everyone laughed.

A pretty girl sat next to Hannah, her auburn hair pulled back tight into a small bun. "My name is Joelle. I'm not quite as talented as Jacie, but I love to dance. I was recently accepted into the San Diego Ballet and Jazz Dance Company."

The introductions ended with a lanky, awkward boy Jacie guessed to be about 13. He moved uncomfortably, not knowing what to do with his shaking hands and oversized feet. "My name's Gregg." He paused. "With three *g*s." He paused again and his voice deepened slightly. "I'm probably going to be a professional bowler if I don't become a lion trainer." Jacie grinned at him—partly out of compassion and partly because his tough guy act was so ridiculous.

Melanie clapped for everyone's attention. As round as she was, she certainly didn't lack for sparkle and enthusiasm. "We're going to assign you prayer partners. These are the people you'll meet with every day to pray together about the team, the trip, and whatever else is on your mind. So as I read off your names, please find your partner."

Melanie looked down at her paper, brushing back a lock of graying black hair. "Okay ... Corey Baxter and Gregg McDonald, Hannah Connor and Joelle Birchwood, Morgan Litney ..."

Jacie waited and scanned the faces of the girls she might be paired with.

"Jacie Noland and Lia Berkowitz . . ."

Jacie's heart skipped. Of all the girls, Lia was probably the boldest and most abrasive. Would she understand Jacie's "can't-we-all-just-get-along" personality?

Lia found Jacie and squatted down next to her, giving her a tight side hug. "I'm soooo glad I'm paired with you. You have the best smile, and you know better than to wear designer sneakers on a missions trip." She flashed a glance at a group of girls nearby.

Jacie couldn't deny she was drawn to Lia's gregariousness. She grinned. "Then I guess it's a good thing I can't afford designer sneakers."

Lia grabbed Jacie's elbow. "Come on. I don't want to stick around here. Wanna find someplace else?"

"Sure." *I always feel weird praying with a bunch of people around anyway.*

"Oh! I have an idea!"

Jacie thought she could almost see the lightbulb on top of Lia's head.

"Let's go pray on the roof!"

Jacie tried to hide her apprehension. "Can we get up there?"

"Only one way to find out. C'mon!" Lia pulled Jacie into an elevator and smacked the button for the top floor.

Lia threw her a wicked grin. "Have you ever heard that if you jump in an elevator that's going down, you get a feeling of gravity-less-ness?"

"I think so, but I've never tried it," Jacie said. "I'm usually more concerned about getting down safely." Jacie glanced out the back of the glass elevator, watching the jungle beneath her grow smaller.

"Let's try!" Lia said.

The elevator bell dinged and Lia immediately pressed the button for the lobby.

Jacie tried not to imagine movies she'd seen of cables breaking, elevators plunging to the ground . . .

"Okay," Lia said, grabbing Jacie's hand. "One . . . two . . . three!" They leaped in unison and landed with a double thump.

"That didn't do much for me," Lia said.

"I guess it doesn't work," Jacie said, although she had to admit it was kind of fun.

Lia climbed up on the elevator bench. "If we jump from here, we'll have more time in the air to feel it. There's room here for you, too," Lia said, her eyes twinkling. Not wanting to disappoint her, Jacie climbed up on the bench.

As the elevator moved downward, the girls leaped in the air, hitting the floor with a colossal thunk. The elevator shuddered and jolted to a stop. The girls stood side by side, giggling as they waited for the doors to open and the new arrival to get on.

Nothing happened.

Lia pressed several buttons.

Jacie waited.

She looked behind them out the glass walls. "Uh. Lia. Are we between two floors?" A wave of dread rose from her stomach to her throat.

Lia pressed her nose against the glass then pulled back, grinning from ear to ear. "Yep!" she announced gleefully.

"This is a good thing?" The last place Jacie wanted to be was stuck in an elevator several floors above the ground.

"Of course it is!"

"Why, exactly?"

"Because I've never been stuck in an elevator before, have you?"

Jacie gave a quick shake of her head.

"What an adventure!" Lia said.

"Okay. So what happens next in the adventure?"

"Well, maybe we wait for our knights in shining armor to rescue us." She leaned dramatically against the back of the elevator, pounding on it with her fists. "Save us! Please, someone help us!"

"Or," Lia struck her Vanna pose again, "we can try this lovely emergency phone."

For no reason, the elevator shuddered again.

"Call," Jacie said.

"Fine." Lia grabbed the receiver and made funny faces while she waited for an answer. Then, "Hi. We're stuck here."

Pause.

"In the elevator."

Another pause.

"No. The el-e-va-tor."

She hung up. "He had a pretty thick accent and had trouble understanding me," she said. "I'm not sure if we'll get rescued or get room service."

"Look." Jacie pointed to a crowd of teens that had formed below them. They waved and pointed up at the glass prison.

Lia's lightbulb popped back on. She pulled out a thick marker and a notebook from her backpack, then scribbled something onto a couple of sheets of paper.

"What are you doing?"

Lia giggled. She held up one of the pages against the glass facing the crowd.

The faces below stared and then looked at each other.

Lia switched the pages a few times until the crowd caught on.

"J!" they shouted.

Lia held up the next page.

"C!" The shouts increased.

Jacie laughed.

"J.C. J.C. J.C." they chanted.

The crowd grew.

"Hand me your notebook, Lia."

Together the girls spelled out *Brio* and even tried *Venezuela*, but the crowd couldn't seem to get the hang of it.

"What's *venzula?*" someone shouted.

A creaking noise turned them around. The doors were opening.

"Are you okay?" asked a voice above them.

The elevator had indeed stalled between floors. Jacie looked up into the faces of two men in uniform and Berk.

"Phooey!" Lia said. "You're not knights. I was at least hoping for room service."

Berk reached down and helped the girls climb up.

"Thanks," Jacie said. The uniformed men returned her smile and said something to each other. They nodded at her, then at Lia, and left, presumably to get someone to fix the elevator.

"Just wondering, Lia," Berk said. "Did you happen to help the elevator get stuck?"

"Not on purpose, Daddy," Lia said.

He shook his head. "It's never on purpose." He gave her cheek a smooch.

"Jacie and I just had so much to pray about," Lia faked.

Berk gave her a suspicious glance.

"Actually, Jacie and I haven't prayed together yet."

"In a stuck elevator? I'd think you'd be praying the whole time," Berk said.

"We were having too much fun," Lia said, smiling at Jacie.

"Go ahead with your dad, Lia," Jacie said. "We'll pray when you get back to the room."

She watched them walk down the corridor arm in arm. *That's what I want, God.* She shook it off and headed to her room in the opposite direction—opting to take the stairs this time. Her giddiness subsided as a strange shadow settled over her. She shut the room door, surprised to find she had the place all to herself. It wouldn't be for long. She unpacked her journal and slumped onto the couch. After writing about her elevator adventure, she let her deeper thoughts come to the surface.

Why did I end up with Lia—the only kid on my team whose dad is here? It seems weird!

unfair that the person I get paired up with not only has a great relationship with her dad, but he's here so I have to watch them. God, it just makes me hurt even more over what I can never have. And yet I'm glad Lia and I were paired up together. She's a lot of fun, and she's definitely got the boldness you need to have on a missions trip. Maybe some of it will rub off on me.

Jacie sighed. In one corner of the journal page, she quickly sketched a father and young daughter holding hands.

Why am I here? I can't even talk to people about Jesus in my own language—let alone Spanish.

Jacie looked at her words. She didn't want to be thinking that way, but it was so hard not to. She'd had a good time tonight, but her purpose for being here wasn't to get stuck in elevators or eat cake at FUAGNEM. There had to be more, but what could that be?

chapter

"Do it again!" Beverly, the drama coach, called inside one of the hotel meeting rooms. She clapped the beat with her hands. "No! Not there, toys. Over there."

Hannah looked up from her journal to see Joelle gliding across the carpeted floor, spinning and leaping with such gracefulness it seemed her feet barely touched the ground. She was perfect as the Spanish Dancer. Hannah had been chosen to be the Princess. And she still couldn't believe it.

> As clumsy as I am, I don't under-
> stand why they chose me for such an
> important part. The Princess is the Eve
> character in the 25-minute drama "The
> Toymaker's Son." All the narration is
> done in Spanish on a CD. So all we have

to do is act out the parts to music.

The other girls on the team said I got the best part, but I have to be on stage pretty much the whole time and in the end, I reject Christ. I feel horrible every time.

My favorite parts are when God creates the world (it's called Toyland) and when the Toymaker (God) sends his Son to redeem Toyland.

It's got all the Bible stuff in it—the creation of Adam and Eve and how the Evil Magician destroys Toyland, separating all the toys from the Toymaker. It makes me cry every time I see the Toymaker trying in vain to get through the barrier to them.

We've been practicing ever since they assigned parts this morning. And it's exhausting! You really get to know people when you watch them in these roles. Sometimes we get a chance to talk a little between scenes. My prayer partner is Joelle, the Spanish Dancer. She is one of the sweetest girls I've ever known. As soon as we met she gave me a big hug and asked what she could be praying about for me. She even has a prayer journal almost exactly like mine. I'm sure we'll have a great—

"Hannah, we're ready for you," Beverly said. "Take your place in the scene where the Evil Magician comes in."

Hannah shoved her journal under her folded sweater and took her position.

"Let's do it with the music this time." Beverly cued up the CD on the portable stereo.

The familiar notes rang out, and almost automatically, Hannah moved with it. *Four steps back . . . Evil Magician comes forward . . . refuse apple . . . look at it again . . . pick apple off tree . . . garden falls.* The music swooned out of tune, and all the garden toys froze. Hannah crouched in an awkward position. *Stay still, stay still,* she pleaded with her body. Her feet started to tremble. A second later, she tumbled over. As she did, she bumped into the Baseball Player, who toppled into the China Doll. The China Doll stumbled into Jacie as the Clown who fell into the Prince and collided with the Nurse. The Nurse tried to catch herself before hitting the Evil Magician, but she pulled him down too. The whole scene collapsed like a line of dominoes.

Everyone groaned and Hannah felt the heat of irritated glares shooting in her direction. She didn't look up from the patterned carpet of the practice room floor.

Beverly sighed and offered a weak smile. "Let's take it from the top."

Practice continued for another couple of hours during which Hannah continued to mess up. It seemed everyone else was learning the parts just fine, and she kept proving her very un-princess-like gracelessness.

"That's it for today, Team 10. Good job, everyone," Beverly said. "Hannah, can I see you for a minute?"

"Yes, Beverly?" Hannah shifted. *Was she going to ask her to not be in the play?*

The instructor placed a hand on Hannah's shoulder and waved toward Joelle, who was gathering her things. "Joelle, would you come here too, please?"

"Sure." Joelle grinned and sashayed over.

The instructor waited until everyone else had left the practice room.

"Hannah, I know you're trying, but ..." she paused. "I thought you could use some extra coaching."

Hannah smiled. "That would be great." She felt relieved she wasn't the only one being singled out. *If Joelle needs extra coaching too, then I certainly can't be that bad. She looked pretty good.*

Beverly continued. "Unfortunately, I have a meeting. But Joelle seems to have caught on pretty quick." She turned to Joelle. "Would you walk Hannah through her steps a few times and show her how to stay in her crouching position without losing her balance?"

"I'd be happy to!" Joelle beamed at Hannah.

"Wonderful!" Beverly grabbed her sweater. "I'll see you both bright and early tomorrow then."

Joelle began to patiently walk through the steps, showing Hannah how to keep her balance by focusing on a distant object.

"Concentrate on the one thing you're looking at, and don't think about your feet or you'll lose it." Joelle laughed. "I learned that at our Christmas recital a few years ago. The whole company froze, and I toppled right onto my bum."

Hannah laughed, but the thought pricked her: *Joelle is being so sweet trying to make me feel better. So why am I so annoyed with her?*

By the time Joelle and Hannah returned to room 512, the other girls were already digging into the pizza that had been delivered.

"You're just in time," Lia said, handing Joelle a slice. A long string of mozzarella stretched across the three feet to Joelle's hand. Hannah reached out to disconnect it.

"Wait!" Lia shouted. "This could be the longest pizza cheese string known to man."

"Maybe we could limbo it!" April suggested.

"Awesome!" Lia agreed. "You go first, Hannah."

"Uh, that's okay. Thanks." Hannah tried to step into the background.

"Quick, it's sagging," said April. The cheese string broke in the middle and landed on the carpet.

The girls moaned and Hannah knelt down with a napkin to pick the remnants out of the shag.

"Aren't y'all just so wiped out from today?" asked Laurilee in her sweet-as-molasses accent. "Acting is such hard work. But I do have to say it's fun being the China Doll. I feel so petite."

"Maybe that's because you *are* petite," smiled Joelle.

"Well, if I keep on eatin' like this, I think that problem will be solved," Laurilee said, holding up her half-eaten slice. "Miss Mercedes, would you mind passin' me a coke, please?"

Mercedes opened the small refrigerator and looked over the soda selection. "There isn't any Coke. How about a Dr Pepper or Mountain Dew?"

"Either one." Her drawl stretched the words like pizza cheese.

Mercedes handed her a can of Dr Pepper.

"Any kind of coke is fine by me." Laurilee popped the top and the soda fizzed.

"But that's not Coke. It's Dr Pepper," Kylie said.

"Right," Laurilee said, her voice almost like a dance. "It's all coke." Laurilee took a long sip. "Course, I can call it soda if y'all want." She pretended to shudder at the thought.

"Nah-ah, girlfriend. It's called pop," insisted Nichole. "Just like the sound it makes."

"Mega-correct," called out Phoebe, giving Nichole a thumbs-up.

"No it doesn't, said Celia. "And besides, if you ask for pop, you might get somebody's grandpa." She turned to Hannah. "What's your preference, Hannah?"

"In Michigan, we called it pop, but in Colorado, everyone says soda."

Jacie sat quietly in the corner observing the conversation. Hannah felt a twinge of concern. It wasn't like Jacie to distance herself.

"Enough!" commanded Lia. She pulled something from her pocket. "I'm tossing this coin. Heads we call it pop, tails we call it soda for the rest of the trip." She flipped the coin in the air, caught it, and slapped on the back of her hand. "Tails!" she announced with a huge grin. "The coin doesn't lie. We call it soda."

Nichole examined Lia, her eyes narrowed. "Let me see that coin," she said, holding out her hand.

"No!" Lia said, beginning to inch toward the door. "It's just a coin."

"You're hidin' something," Nichole said. "Girls. Get her!"

In a flash, six girls piled onto Lia. Phoebe finally pried the coin out of her tightly clutched palm.

"It's a two-tailed coin!" she announced.

"Wow," Lia's muffled voice said. "I wonder how—"

The rest of her question disappeared as she again vanished under a pile of girls.

Knock. Knock.

"Lia? It's Dad." A muted voice came from the other side of the door. Lia called from under the pileup, "Dad, save me! Save me!"

Nichole rushed to the door and flung it open. "She's buried there," she pointed.

Mr. Berkowitz smirked. "Well, Lia. I have a feeling you probably deserve whatever you're getting."

"Thanks for the vote of confidence, Dad," Lia said, tunneling out from the squirming bodies.

Berk tousled his daughter's hair affectionately. "Am I right, girls?"

"Yes!" the dispersing pile shouted.

"I hate to break up the party, but I need to borrow Lia." He turned to his daughter. "We told Mom we'd call her tonight."

"Sure," Lia said, slipping on her shoes. She made a face at her friends. "I can tell her all about my evil roommates."

Hannah watched Jacie as they left. The other girls resumed their conversation, but Jacie excused herself to the adjoining bedroom.

"Jacie, are you okay?" Hannah asked, following her friend into the room and plopping herself down on the bed, where Jacie lay facing the window.

"Yeah." Jacie turned around. "I just feel sad for some reason. Like there's a gaping hole inside."

"Are you homesick?" Hannah had already been missing her family.

"No. It's just . . ." Jacie paused. "Berk's a great guy, don't you think?"

Hannah nodded slowly. "Well, yeah. But he's kind of old. And *married!*"

"I don't mean that, you goof!" Jacie bopped Hannah with a pillow. "I was thinking that he's a really good dad."

"Oh. Yeah. Of course," Hannah said, pretending not to be embarrassed. She nodded and blinked. "He and Lia seem really close. It makes me miss my dad to see them together. I . . . oh." Hannah stopped short.

After a long moment of silence, Jacie said, "It makes me miss what I've never really had."

"But, Jacie, you have a dad. He's just farther away than most. He still loves you."

Jacie gave a half-grin. "I know—but I don't think I'm that important to him."

"Sure you are. The distance just makes it harder for him to show it."

"He could do more if he tried. He could have come on this trip like Berk."

Hannah knew enough to realize that would never happen.

Jacie continued, "It's fun visiting him in California and doing stuff together. But he doesn't call enough to know much about my life. Sometimes I feel like rent-a-kid—we just hang out when he feels like having a daughter. Otherwise—"

Hannah couldn't imagine life without her dad. She put her head down on Jacie's for a moment and sighed. "I'm sorry" was all she could think to say.

• • •

After the evening worship, Berk gathered Team 10 for another meeting. He held up a hand to quiet the chattering. "We're going to practice giving our testimonies since we'll be sharing them in Venezuela."

"What if we don't know any Spanish?" Jacie asked.

"We'll have an interpreter. But sometimes saying it in English is hard enough."

"No argument there," Jacie said.

Melanie spoke up, "We'll get with our prayer partners and tell them how we became Christians."

"But I've been a Christian my whole life. That's a pretty short story," muttered Kylie.

"Right," Melanie said. "Most of us have probably had that same experience. I became a Christian when I was five. But I can still share how the Lord has impacted my life, how He's been faithful to me, or how I've grown since accepting Christ."

"Can we share what brought us on this trip?" asked Celia.

"That's easy. A plane," said Corey.

Melanie rolled her eyes, but the smile stayed on her face. "Of course, Celia. Just share what's on your mind."

Berk turned and smiled at Jacie. "I know this can be a little scary for some of you who haven't done this before. So before we break up, let's hear from some of you who have shared your faith. Does anyone have any experiences to share?"

"I do." Hannah almost jumped up. "I love to share my faith. And I'm pretty comfortable with it. Even with people I don't know."

"Great. What do you say?" asked Berk.

"Well," Hannah said, clasping her hands on her lap, "I tell them that the world has fooled them with many lies. They may think they are happy, but they really aren't. I use the Bible a lot. Verses like 'For all have sinned and fallen short of the glory of God.' It's kind of a reminder to people that because of their sin they deserve to go to hell, but it is only by God's grace that He died for us and offers us freedom from sin."

Hannah paused to take a breath, but Berk said, "Thanks, Hannah. Anyone have other thoughts?"

Joelle started shyly, "I don't have the experience Hannah does and, well, the truth is I'm pretty scared about it. I've been praying a lot about it lately—especially once I knew I was coming on this trip." She laughed nervously. "Last week at cheerleading camp, one of the girls on my squad told us she was going through a tough time with her parents' divorce. And I felt God prodding me to talk with her."

She stared at the waterfall, remembering.

"I told her about a hard time in my life, and she asked how I made it through. I told her about my relationship with God and how, even though things aren't perfect, just knowing that He loves me and that He's there got me through it. We talked a lot after that and by Friday, she asked me if I would pray with her to accept Christ."

"That's wonderful, Joelle," said Melanie. "It's important for all of us to remember that our job isn't to argue people into the kingdom. God has prepared the people He wants to reach. He's the one changing people's hearts, not us. We only have to be willing to share and leave the heart-changing up to God."

Joelle smiled. "I was just telling her about my Best Friend—which He is."

April sat up straighter. "I think people respond when you share your own struggles. Sometimes people are turned off to Christianity because Christians act like they have perfect lives."

"Or like they are better than everyone else," someone said.

Hannah swallowed. *Was that how my comment came across?*

Mercedes said, "The way you describe it, Joelle, it sounds like something I could do. I've been worried that I would have to be like Billy Graham or something."

Laughter around the circle demonstrated that many others understood. Mercedes continued, "I figured I'd have to know all the right answers and come up with great illustrations, but it sounds like you were just . . ." She paused to think of the right word. ". . . real. And that's all."

"Well," Berk leaned forward in his chair. "How about we get with our prayer partners now and practice being 'real'?"

Hannah thought that judging from people's reactions, Joelle had been more helpful than she had. *If Berk had allowed me to continue, I'd have hit all those points too.*

But part of her wasn't quite sure that was true.

chapter 6

Jacie moved down the aisle of yet another plane, trying to push her fears aside. *What a witness it would be,* she thought, *if a whole plane full of kids headed for the mission field crashed.* She shook her head, trying to rid her mind of the nagging idea. Once she knew the entire plane would be filled completely with three teams of Brio kids, the thought had been recurring. What news that would make! She could see clips of kids crying and news stories about how these kids loved Jesus—

"Sit here!" Becca said, yanking on Jacie's "Nerve to Serve" shirt.

Jacie dropped into the empty seat and put her pack on the floor in front of her. "Thanks. This plane is nuts."

"Yeah. Cool, huh? Kind of electric," Becca said, looking at the teal shirts swarming over seats.

Jacie shrugged.

"Scared?" Becca asked.

She nodded.

"Well. Stop it. Nothing's going to happen."

Jacie took a deep breath, willing herself to believe it. She buckled her seatbelt and tightened it. "I feel like I haven't talked to you in forever."

"I know," Becca agreed. "But I knew you'd be fine without me. Especially when I saw you leading cheers from the stuck elevator! Only you, Jacie Noland."

"You mean only Lia. She's the one who did it." Jacie kicked her pack under the seat in front of her. "How do you like your team?"

"Team 12 rocks!" Becca said, loud enough to elicit cheers from the rear of the plane. "I get so pumped being around people who are on fire for God."

Jacie shook her head. Becca had never needed other people to get her excited about anything.

Becca eyed her curiously. "What are you thinking?"

"You belong on this trip. Everyone here belongs on this trip. I just don't think *I* do."

Becca gave a frustrated sigh. "Of course you belong here. Everyone loves you! They always do."

"They're on a missions trip. They're *supposed* to like everyone."

Becca smirked. "But not everyone has their name chanted by crowds of people everywhere."

Jacie fought a smirk. Ever since the elevator adventure, the "J.C." chant greeted her whenever she entered a room.

"Becca, the other day we practiced giving our testimonies to each other." Her voice took on a strained tone. "I said, 'I became a Christian when I was six. It's been good.' And then I stopped. What else do you say?"

"How about how you've grown? Or what God's done in your life and how He has been faithful? You've talked to me about those things a hundred times."

"But it's different when I'm talking to a Christian friend than when

I'm in front of a hundred people wearing sombreros and forced grins."

"I don't think they wear sombreros in Venezuela."

"They don't?" Jacie sighed, then came back, her voice rising in pitch. "That's not really the point anyway, and you know it. It's that I don't want the responsibility of knowing someone's eternity depends on how I come off . . ."

"You've been hanging around Hannah too long," Becca said. "You've got to relax, Jace."

"I know."

"You don't need to be scared. God will give you the words when the time comes. You only need to be willing to step out on the limb."

"Until the limb breaks and I fall off."

"Then you just have to trust that He'll catch you."

"You haven't met my team. I'm not as bold or articulate—" Jacie stopped short, noticing Hannah standing at the front of the plane snapping pictures of the flight attendants.

Becca followed her glance.

"She'll be handing out tracts in a moment," Jacie said wistfully.

"You don't have to be like Hannah."

"Hey, what does 'J.C.' stand for anyway?" a voice behind them called. "Jolly Clown? Juicy Crumbs? Oh . . . I know! Jell-O Cube. That's your real name, right?" Gregg laughed and snorted. "Oh, I think I'm gonna be sick."

Becca ignored the interruption. "Sorry. What were you saying?" she asked Jacie.

"That everyone else on my team is more articulate."

Gregg moaned behind her. "Where are those . . . things? Those baggy thingamajobbers?"

"Well, most of them," Jacie whispered.

● ● ●

Exhausted, Jacie couldn't sleep. The bus driver shifted into a lower gear, and the stench of exhaust poured through the windows. Her stomach turned. She stared out the window into the darkness, hoping for a glimpse of the wonder of being in a foreign country. *Caracas*. She still couldn't get over the fact that she was here, that the plane didn't crash into the crystal blue waters of the Caribbean. They'd zipped through customs, waited forever for their luggage, and boarded a bus. Now they were on their way to the hotel. Most of the kids on the bus leaned against each other, deep in sleep, their mouths hanging open. Becca, her head in Jacie's lap, had fallen asleep within three minutes of leaving the airport.

The tortured bus groaned up one hill and down another. Lights climbed into the darkness, twinkling on the hills surrounding the road. To Jacie it looked like a fairy city, with so many lights on the hills.

When the bus finally lurched to a stop, sleepy kids stumbled into the darkness, a mob of zombies waiting to receive their room assignments.

Hannah found Jacie and tugged on her arm. "We're in the same suite with our Miami roommates and other Team 10 girls!"

"Great," Jacie said, not bothering to stifle a yawn. "Let's get up there and go to bed."

The tiny elevator, which could hold only two girls and their luggage, slowly creaked its way up to the 18th floor. When they had arrived at the suite, Hannah knocked on the door and Joelle threw it open. "Come in! Welcome to our new home!" she said, sweeping her arm wide.

"Wow," Jacie said, scanning the living room in disbelief. "It's like stepping back into the '70s."

"What do you think of the mega-wild carpet?" Phoebe asked. "I used to have hair this color."

Hannah looked at her. "You had orange hair?"

Phoebe shrugged. "Not for long. After a while it felt like my head was rusting."

Lia popped out of a narrow hallway. "Three bedrooms, two people each," she announced.

"How cute," called Mercedes. "There's a little cubby off the kitchen."

"Y'all, I don't think there's enough beds for all of us," Laurilee said. "I s'pose we can pull out the couches in the living room."

Jacie circled the living room. It felt icky. She wrapped her arms around herself.

Dingy, worn furniture looked almost gummy. The faded art on the walls clashed loudly with the wild pattern of the musty drapes. Combined with the orange shag carpet, it was an artist's nightmare.

A warm night breeze blew through the screenless window, beckoning Jacie to come look out. She peered down, her stomach clenching at how far down the 18 floors fell. She quickly stepped back from the dark hand that would pull her to the ground.

"Um hm, take a look at this view," Nichole said, waving the girls to the little window on the other side of the room. They gathered around, looking at the lights below. The drop was much farther on this side.

Joelle stood on the couch, cleared her throat, and waved her arms. "Hey, everybody! Listen up! Melanie asked me to tell you guys that this place is on water restriction. They bring water in on trucks and pump it into storage tanks. So we only have water from seven to nine in the morning and from five to midnight in the evening unless we run out sooner. We can only flush the toilet, use the sinks, or take showers during those times. Don't drink any water except the bottled stuff we have in the kitchen. Also, Venezuela's sewer system has problems. So we can't flush toilet paper—*ever*."

"What do we do with it?" Laurilee's nose looked like it might crinkle into itself.

"Throw it in the trash can."

Well, this will make the next 10 days a real adventure, won't it?

● ● ●

Jacie woke and stretched under her scratchy sheets, blinking the sleep from her eyes. Forgetting momentarily where she was, she scanned the dim room. The first light of day peeked through the thin curtains, drenching the room in soft gray.

The air felt heavy—not like the thin, high altitude air in Colorado. She breathed in its dense warmth as she silently slid off the pullout couch, being careful not to disturb the evenly breathing bodies that lay around her. After rummaging through her suitcase for a sketchbook, Jacie sat in front of the kitchen window. She stared at a city that looked like it never slept. From her perch, she had a bird's-eye view of the cement-slabbed buildings and traffic. A blanket of smog veiled the downtown area. City lights dotted the dim morning landscape. Metal bars on the building windows protected the occupants.

Jacie remembered the day that Hannah brought a Venezuelan guidebook to school. At the lunch table, the four of them pored over the pages, examining each picture. Solana sat back, pretending to be uninterested but occasionally throwing out snide comments. "Look at that shopping mall—I thought you were going to the jungle or something. What kind of missions trip is this?"

Becca swatted Solana. "There are more people to minister to in a city than in the jungle, silly."

Hannah pointed out pictures of an apartment building with bars—so much like what Jacie looked at now. "It's like they live in cages," Hannah said.

"It must be really unsafe," Jacie said, trying not to think about a city that had to barricade all of its windows.

Hannah shook her head, as though tossing off a burden. "The bars remind me that they are captives—imprisoned by their sin." She looked up at Jacie. "Doesn't this make you want to go, knowing how these lost people need Christ?"

Guilt washed over Jacie. She felt so insensitive. Of course she wanted to go—to learn and especially to do something tangible to make life easier for these struggling people. But she never felt as burdened for the lost as Hannah did, no matter how much she tried. And, whenever she thought about that, she felt so ashamed.

Even now, with the warm breeze flooding her face through the open window, she prayed that God would make her more compassionate.

Jacie pulled her charcoal pencil from the top of the sketchbook and began to draw the scene below. As her hands moved across the page, she realized she was seeing deeper into the city. The beauty became more apparent—a massive mountain range loomed as a backdrop to the skyline. As the rising sun began to cast shadows over the jagged ridges, Jacie blended, smudged, and smoothed the grays to match the shadowed peaks. She became immersed in her drawing—entering a world that consisted of only her art and her soul. At times like this, her hand seemed to move of its own accord. Eventually, Jacie heard the faraway sound of the other girls waking up, showers starting, and travel alarm clocks beeping.

"Jacie. That's amazing!" The shrill voice over Jacie's shoulder caused her to jump. "I didn't know you could draw."

Self-consciously, Jacie held the sketchbook to her chest, more concerned about strangers seeing into her secret world than about getting charcoal on her sleepshirt. "I'm just doodling."

"That's not doodling," Mercedes said.

"Jacie," Hannah called from the hallway entrance over the din of hair dryers, showers, and morning chatter. "Can I borrow your sunscreen?"

"Sure," Jacie answered. "I'll get it."

Jacie retrieved the sunscreen and scuttled to Hannah's room, tossing it on her bed. "I can't believe you actually forgot something. I thought you were the most thorough packer ever."

Hannah slathered the lotion on her arms. "Well, I didn't actually forget it. But it looked like you needed rescuing."

Jacie grinned. "Thanks."

"Even though I'll never understand why you keep your gift a secret."

"It's hard to explain." Jacie had never really understood it herself. As a little girl, she wanted to show everyone her drawings and paintings. Maybe the change came when she realized that her art represents the deepest parts of her—private depths of thoughts and feelings—leaving her vulnerable to others. What Mercedes might describe as merely a pretty skyline with mountains, was actually much more—her fears, guilt, inadequacies, and hopes. "It's like exposing my soul," she mustered.

Hannah nodded, concentrating on covering her knees with sunscreen.

"So, not that I care, but why are you using my sunscreen if you brought your own?" Jacie asked.

Hannah bit the inside of her cheek. "Because I asked to borrow it, I have to use it. Otherwise my asking for it would be deceitful."

Jacie stifled a laugh. The culture around her could change, but Hannah would always be the same.

● ● ●

"We're heading down for breakfast," Jill called as Jacie tried to tame her curls that had gone wild in the humidity.

"Okay!" She looked in the mirror. "I give up anyway."

"I'm starving," Kylie said as Jacie joined the group. "This better be a good breakfast. I'm hoping for pancakes and sausage."

"I want grits," Laurilee said.

"Dream on," Lia said to both of them. "We'll be lucky to get oatmeal."

When the girls entered the dining area, they each took a damp plate from a tall stack. Several men stood behind a long table serving what looked like some sort of unnatural variation on the scrambled eggs and toast theme.

"Eggs should be okay," Lia said over her shoulder.

"You sure those are eggs?" said Phoebe. "They look like some kind of sloppy Jell-O."

Jacie gulped. Whatever the soupy, clumpy, whitish stuff was, it certainly didn't look palatable. A grinning Venezuelan server dumped some onto her plate. A pool of milky water spread across the plate, fleeing the mass. Jacie took a couple of pieces of petrified white bread. She held them up to the girls. "Toast?"

Lia shrugged, adding little tubs of jam to her plate.

The girls sat down at a round table. After Lia prayed, they all sat, staring down at their "breakfast."

"You first, Hannah," Jacie said, knowing Hannah was accustomed to questionable food. Being the oldest of five kids, she sampled food, finished off her little sister's half-eaten dinner, and tested milk to see if it was sour.

Hannah scooped a forkful of the solid part into her mouth, chewed a few times, and swallowed with a big gulp.

Laurilee shuddered.

"It's . . . edible," Hannah said, scooping up more.

Jacie dropped her toast onto the table. It bounced twice. "I don't know about this. I might break a tooth."

Jill took her piece and broke it with both hands. Chunks broke off and crumbs exploded across the table. "It's a giant crouton."

Celia rolled her eyes. "Great. Egg soup and croutons for breakfast."

"Not quite pancakes and sausage," Kylie said, moving eggs around in the puddle on her plate.

"Or grits," Laurilee said, sighing.

"Well," Joelle held up her toast, "I guess it's part of the experience."

True, Jacie thought. She held up her toast and tapped it against Joelle's. "To the missions trip!"

"Here, here," called the others, raising their own pieces above the center of the table.

"I've never toasted with toast before," Jacie said, smiling.

chapter

Today is our first day of ministry. I'm so excited! The bus is taking us to a school on the outskirts of Caracas. Mud slides destroyed it not long ago, and they're trying to rebuild it. I'm glad we'll be able to play with the kids some. I miss my sisters and brothers.

The bus trundled through city streets and over crowded freeways where men walked the lanes between vehicles, peddling their wares. The bus lumbered up a mountain where villages of stacked homes clung to the steep hillside like red-and-gray LEGO blocks.

Jacie leaned against Hannah's shoulder, her breath slow and even. Hannah stared out the window. On one side of the bus the ocean rippled a silver blue in the sun. On the other, a city bustled with activity. People moved along the sidewalks in front of storefronts labeled with bold black letters. Some people looked grumpy, others walked with purpose, chatting on cell phones, but mostly, they looked bored. All seemed oblivious of what they had grown accustomed to—the layers of decaying colorful paint peeling off the walls and windows with wrought iron grates over them.

The bus shifted gears and turned onto a narrow street. They passed street after street of houses built right next to each other, sharing the walls of the houses on either side. Shops occasionally appeared between two homes. *So many shoe stores for Jacie*, Hannah thought. *It's a good thing she's asleep.*

The farther they drove, the more shabby and dusty the streets became. The bus finally groaned and hissed to a stop next to a small, run-down park in the town square. Curious Venezuelans eyed the bus. Many men stood about, lazily smoking cigarettes and exchanging glances. *Why are they here?* she wondered. *It must be a holiday.*

Jacie moved and stretched next to her. "Are we there?"

Hannah nodded.

Jacie looked past her out the window. "Wow. Look at all those men." She looked at her watch. "It's too early for lunch. Do you think maybe they don't have jobs?"

The thought hadn't even occurred to Hannah. *They must be filled with worry about supporting their families.* A wave of compassion swept over her, and she leaned out the window to give them a cheery wave. One of the men called out in Spanish and blew her a kiss. In her hurry to duck back inside the bus, she smacked the back of her head on the window. "Ow!"

Jacie laughed. "That's what you get for flirting with strange men."

"I'm not flirting," Hannah protested as she rubbed the back of her head.

"Let's go!" Berk called from the front of the bus.

The already excited bus chatter went up a notch.

Hannah's heart jumped. *This is it, God. I'm going to work hard for You today. If I need to, I'll stop everything to tell someone about You. I'm completely and totally Yours this trip. Teach me, God. Teach me so much that I'll never forget.*

She followed her 30 teammates into the hot Venezuelan sunshine, her insides twitching with eagerness.

"This is Hank," announced Berk, when the group had congregated on the sidewalk. "He's been a missionary in Venezuela for 20 years, and he'll be heading up our work project today."

"Hi, everyone!" Hank said, with a long, sweeping wave.

"Hi, Hank!" the team responded.

The chunky man seemed exceptionally cheerful, and with a scruff of white beard, he reminded Jacie a bit of a young Santa Claus. "Glad to have you here!" he bellowed. "Are you ready to work?"

"Yeah!" the team answered in unison.

"Good! Let's go, then!"

Hank moved up a steep hill with the team trailing behind. As they walked, Hank told stories about the people who lived in the disheveled shacks on each side of the narrow street and the ways that he and other missionaries were trying to reach out to them.

"Esperanza lives up there," he said, pointing to a crumbling one-room shanty, a piece of tin set on top as a flimsy roof. "She lost her husband and two oldest children in the mud slides. A few months later, her remaining child died in a fire."

Hannah watched the woman hanging out her wash. *My mom wouldn't even use those as rags,* she thought. As she zoomed in with her camera for a photograph, snapshots of her mom, dad, and five little brothers and sisters flashed through her mind. She couldn't imagine losing her entire family. *How does Esperanza go on living?*

"Alberto and Maria live over there—" Hank continued with his narrative.

The uphill climb in the hot, sticky weather began to take its toll on Hannah's energy. Others reached for their water bottles, wiping hands across their damp foreheads. Hank stopped the group for a welcome rest in front of a 150-yard-wide culvert.

"Believe it or not," he said in a booming voice so everyone could hear, "this gully used to be a village before the mud slides came through."

Hannah did a double take. She couldn't imagine this muddy gorge, now stripped of all life, as a neighborhood.

"Rain poured down for 14 days. Mount Avila," he said, pointing toward a stubby-topped mountain, "could no longer hold the mass of water. In the middle of the night, the peak collapsed. The saturated mountaintop, combined with the massive rainfall, created surging rivers of mud that demolished villages on their way to the sea. You can't even see where the houses once were."

The group stared silently, unable to grasp the ramifications of such tragedy.

Joelle cleared her throat. "How many people . . . um—"

"It's hard to even guess how many died," Hank offered. "The areas were densely populated slums that housed mostly unregistered residents. Some guess the death toll to be as high as 200,000."

Two hundred thousand. Hannah's mind reeled. *That's more than the entire population of Copper Ridge.* Hank went on to explain how some bodies were found with babies still in their arms. Hannah didn't want to hear any more. *God, how many families . . . how many people died without knowing You?*

The group continued the climb up the hill. Complaints about the heat and the hike ceased, transformed into a somber silence.

Suddenly, a thought popped into Hannah's mind. She wove through her teammates to catch up with Hank. "What an opportunity to share Christ during this time of tragedy."

He nodded. "Yes, but the truth is before you can convince people they need Christ, you must meet their immediate needs. These people are just trying to survive—find enough food to make it through the day. If you start telling them that all they need is Jesus, church, and a Bible, you've lost them."

Joelle sidled up to the other side of Hank. "That must be exhausting work."

"It has certainly taken an emotional toll on my family," Hank said. "My wife and daughter left for the States for a three-month furlough yesterday. My son and I will join them soon. It will be a much-needed break for all of us."

"How old is your son?" Hannah asked.

"Jared is nearly 24. You'll meet him later today when he comes to help out. In fact, we're staying in your hotel until we return to the States."

"Watch out for the roaches," joked Joelle.

Hank chuckled. "Trust me, compared to how most of these people live, your run-down, roach-infested hotel is a palace."

● ● ●

Hannah felt the dust clinging to her tongue. She washed it away with a swig of water as the group walked up another dusty hill. Even living in the mountains of Colorado hadn't prepared her for this hike.

Just when she felt she couldn't go on, they arrived at the school. Hannah had never seen anything like it. Even before the mud slides, the school couldn't have been much. The brick walls sagged under their own weight. A warped tin roof rattled in the breeze. A fine dust collected in the corners with trash and broken concrete pieces. Five small classrooms burst at the seams with nearly 40 students crammed into each.

Hank led them upstairs where he handed out wheelbarrows and shovels that lined the cracked walls. He motioned down an open hallway. "We'll be cleaning out these two classrooms that we haven't been able to use."

Immediately, the group set to work. Despite the intense humidity, they packed wheelbarrows with rubble and pushed them outside to the growing refuse pile. They sang songs and told stories. Morgan shared about living in Europe. Laurilee taught them how to speak Southern.

Wishing for the umpteenth time she had thought to bring work gloves, Hannah dumped a wheelbarrow of debris then wiped her dirty hands on her smudged overalls.

"I have to admit," Jacie said, handing Hannah a water bottle, "as hot and tiring as this is, it's fun."

Hannah nodded, her mouth full of water. But still, she longed to get among the people—to fulfill her assigned task: *Winning people for Jesus.*

Joelle dropped her shovel nearby. "Isn't this wonderful? Soon there will be no more crowded classrooms. How rewarding is that? Even after we get home, our work will still be appreciated."

Corey piled shattered bricks into a nearby wheelbarrow. "You're crazy. We should all feel guilty."

Hannah choked on her water. "Guilty? Why?"

"Because of us, these poor kids will keep getting homework."

"Hey, y'all. Lunchtime!" sang Laurilee, carrying a pile of stubby rolls smeared with peanut butter and jelly, baked earlier that day in Caracas. A tub of Wet Wipes for cleanup balanced precariously on her bent arm.

"Great. I'm starved," said Gregg, nabbing a sandwich with a grubby hand.

"Eww, take a Wet Wipe first," insisted Laurilee.

Corey took a huge bite out of his lunch. "I don't know when PB&J ever tasted so good," he said through a mouthful of sandwich.

"Well, you can still mind your manners and not talk with your mouth full," Morgan said dryly.

"Oh, does this bother you?" he asked, opening his stuffed mouth to display its half-chewed contents.

"Gross!" Morgan aimed her water bottle at Corey, gave it a firm squeeze, and drenched his face and shirt.

Corey snatched his own bottle and squeezed back. Morgan ducked, and the stream of water splattered April's face. April shook her head like a dog, spraying the kids around her. She grabbed a milk jug of water and began unscrewing the cap.

"You wouldn't—" Corey said, his eyes widening.

"You wanna bet?" April flashed an evil grin. "Hold him down, girls."

Jacie, Joelle, Mercedes, and Lia grabbed him, each pinning a squirming limb to the floor.

"He-e-e-lp!" bellowed Corey. "Someone protect me from these wild women!"

"Sorry, Corey," said Gregg. "You're on your own. I don't mess with cuckoo birds."

"*Cuckoo birds?*" said Morgan, standing behind him with her own water bottle. She shot a look to Lia. Lia nodded in response.

Corey's wails were joined by high-pitched screams from Gregg as Morgan and Lia dumped the milk jug over his head.

Hannah stood to one side, unsure about what to do and appalled at their lack of discipline. Everyone had armed themselves with water bottles, shooting anything that moved. Dripping faces, gurgling laughter, and sopping ponytails filled the dusty classroom. "Eeek!" "Oops!" "Watch it!" "Get him, April!"

Hannah waved her arms to try to get their attention. "Stop it, you guys! We can't waste the water. It's a precious commodity." In a moment she, too, was drenched.

Corey handed Hannah a spare water bottle. "Arm yourself, tall one," he said in a stilted Native-American accent. "The white men have come to soak and destroy."

"No!" Hannah threw up her arms, the water bottle in her hand letting fly a stream of water onto herself. "Seriously, we're supposed to be working!"

"Yeah. And I need help outside," a voice commanded, abruptly ending the chaos. A lanky man in his early 20s stood in the doorway staring coldly at them from pale blue eyes.

"Who are you?" Gregg asked, as though ready to punch the guy who broke up their game.

"I'm Jared. And unlike you, I'm here to work."

"We're here—"

"Why don't you boys grab some shovels and do some real work?"

The edge in his voice demanded obedience. The teens were silent as Corey and Gregg followed Jared out the door.

"Boy, someone got up on the wrong side of bed," Joelle murmured.

"And he's a missionary!" Kylie exclaimed.

Berk appeared just as the dripping group began to work again.

"Did it rain and I missed it?" he joked.

"Consider yourself lucky," said Hannah, wringing out her ponytail.

"Hannah, you're just the person I need!"

Hannah perked up, ready for whatever Berk asked her to do.

"Melanie isn't feeling well. I've told her to go back to the bus so she can lie down. Could you take over watching the backpacks for the afternoon?" Since most of the backpacks held cameras and money, one person was needed to guard them.

"Um, sure," Hannah said, disappointed. "Unless someone else would like to do it." *I could be of better use being in charge of keeping a work team focused and on task.*

"Thanks a lot, Hannah. I appreciate it," Berk said.

Hannah went to the small cement-walled room and slumped into a metal folding chair in the corner. One of the chair legs splayed out, forcing her to hold herself at an angle. Holding her chin in her hands, she looked around the room. It looked an awful lot like a jail cell. *Well, here I am, God. Backpack security. Not quite the ministry You'd want me to have.*

Through the barred window, she saw children playing tag outside. Some of her team members joined them. The children shrieked happily as the teenagers chased them.

Hannah drummed her fingers on her cheeks.

God, I'm not doing anything. You could send me someone to minister to.

Maybe one of the kids would get hurt and she could help.

Hannah! What are you thinking?

What else could she do? Her mother told of an experience she had helping a woman give birth on an airplane. Hannah thought that sounded so heroic. She could probably do that. That would make a great story for her "thank you for your support" letter. She searched out the window for a pregnant woman.

"*Buenos días!*" Hannah looked up to see an elderly woman wearing a long gray skirt and a multicolored smock. Strands of gray hair escaped her long braid. Deep creases lined her face. But her toothy grin, yellowed yet pleasant, seemed bigger than all the rest of her. "Luisa," she said, pounding her chest with the palm of her hand.

The woman jabbered in her native tongue a mile a minute. She fluttered her hands about freely, using them to demonstrate her words. She kept reaching for imaginary things in the air and making circular motions on her stomach. Although Hannah knew better, all she could think of was her daydream of helping a woman give birth.

A better thought came to her and excitement rushed into her heart. *This is it! Thank You, Jesus!* Hannah reached for her backpack and pulled out her Bible.

She tapped the Bible, then her own heart. "Jesus. In my heart."

Then she tapped the Bible and pointed at Luisa. "Jesus. You need Jesus in your heart."

Luisa nodded and babbled on, waving her arms for emphasis.

"You need Jesus," Hannah said, smiling, touching her Bible. She opened her Bible to John 3:16. "Jesus loves you."

Luisa's parched, dry face peered at the Bible. She stared at it a moment, then grinned widely.

She's getting it! Hannah thought, joy surging through her.

"*Es una Biblia! Jesus es mi salvador también!*"

Hannah caught "Bible" and "Jesus," but wasn't sure what else the woman said.

Luisa took the Bible and held it over her heart and closed her eyes. She did a little spinning dance, her eyes still closed. Then she stopped. Suddenly, the woman's eyes widened as though she remembered something. She said something else Hannah didn't understand, handed

croutons for breakfast

59

Hannah the Bible, and then disappeared from the room as quickly as she'd entered.

What was that? Hannah thought. Before she could sort it out, she heard the approaching voices of her teammates. Jacie and Corey came in with a handful of other dirty, sweat-drenched kids.

"Whew!" Corey said, wiping the sweat off his forehead, leaving a dirty smudge in its place. "This is tough work."

Jacie rummaged through her backpack for her water bottle. "Yeah, but you can tell the people are so appreciative. It's in their eyes and smiles."

Hannah kept quiet. She didn't want to draw attention to the fact that she'd been sitting around in a relatively cool place doing nothing the entire afternoon.

Jacie took a swig of her water. "So, Hannah—"

Luisa flurried back into the room, this time with three laughing, chattering women.

Luisa held out a thick, whitish pastry-looking dish. It looked glossy, almost rubbery, and Hannah couldn't tell if it was egg or frosting.

"Venga. Coma," Luisa said, holding the cake toward Hannah. She pantomimed eating. The other women stood behind her, expectant. One began pouring a light-colored soda into small plastic cups.

April looked at her wide-eyed. "What is it?" she murmured under her breath so only Hannah could hear.

Hannah didn't know what to do. She couldn't refuse—but she didn't know if it was something that would make her sick. Luisa laid the dish on a table and began carving it with a plastic knife. Hannah could finally see what it was—cheese. Luisa handed her a piece and she bit into it. Rich and creamy fresh cheese. She smiled at Luisa and rubbed her stomach. "Yum!" she said. "Better than any cheese I've ever had at home."

Luisa and the other women nodded happily.

Seeing that Hannah didn't keel over and die, the rest of the group enthusiastically joined in the snack.

Hannah noticed Luisa's torn, discolored smock. She rummaged through her backpack and pulled out a spare sweatshirt. It wasn't anything nice—just a gray fleece with "Camp Bosheegen" emblazoned on the front in faded red. She held it out to the woman.

"For you, for you," she said, pointing at the shirt, then at Luisa.

The woman looked at the shirt, confused, and then laughed. She took the shirt and held it up to her generously bosomed chest. The sweatshirt was obviously too small for her to wear. Hannah's cheeks flushed. *Have I offended her?* But the woman continued to laugh as she folded the garment and placed it back in Hannah's bag.

"*Gracias, hija.*" Luisa grinned her tooth-missing grin and patted Hannah's cheek. "*Gracias.*"

Hannah racked her brain, trying to think of something she could offer the woman, this sister in Christ. Guilt swept through her. Her financial supporters didn't donate money so she could go to a foreign country and eat a poor woman's cheese.

"Isn't this wonderful?" Jacie asked, holding up her hunk of cheese.

Hannah gave a quick nod.

"What's wrong?"

"This is such a sacrifice for them. I should be showing Christ's love and generosity *to them*, not the other way around."

"If God wants to give you a gift, why not accept it?"

Hannah pursed her lips into a thin line. Again, she could see Luisa dancing with joy just to hold a Bible. *Because it's not my turn. It was Luisa's and I blew it.*

chapter 8

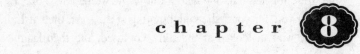

I love it when I can afford a new outfit from Raggs by Razz. For a moment, I actually like who I am and how I look.

Today is different. My hair is dirty, my face smudged with soot, my dingy work clothes caked in mud—but I feel great! I love who God made me to be. For once, how I look is completely unimportant. The hard work to help those kids brought me more joy than any new outfit ever will. I'll never forget those windows filled with round, brown faces. Or how excited those kids were when they came into the courtyard to play with us. What a different perspective on what's really important in life!

The bus squeaked to a stop at the bottom of the hotel's steep driveway. Corey let out a whoop. "Time to hit the pool!"

Jacie slid her journal into her backpack.

"Jacie," Berk called. "Would you please take the water jugs to the dining hall?"

Jacie smiled, taking the plastic water containers from Berk. "Sure!"

Gregg rushed up the aisle. "I'll help you, Jacie!"

"Uh, thanks!" Jacie said.

They said nothing to each other all the way through the courtyard to the dining hall and even after dropping off the water bottles. Gregg hung behind her right shoulder as if attached by a leash. Jacie wondered what in the world she was expected to do. She felt like zigzagging through the clumps of kids to see what Gregg would do.

"Jaaaacieeeeee!" someone pounced on her. It could only be—

"Becca!" Jacie spun around and gave Becca a huge hug. "I'm so glad to see you. I swear it's been a month!"

"You doin' okay?" Becca swung a plastic baseball bat—a prop from the day's performance.

Jacie nodded, showing Becca the dirt under her nails. "You wouldn't believe how hard we worked . . . How was your show?"

"Awesome. Maybe we could catch up tonight." Becca peered around Jacie's shoulder at Gregg. "Hi, I'm Becca."

"Hi. I'm Gregg. With three gs. I'm on Jacie's team. I helped her carry water bottles. Now we're going back upstairs." The words sounded stilted, as if he read from a script.

Becca gave Jacie a strange look, then said to Gregg, "Weren't you gagging behind us on the plane?"

"Oh. Yeah."

"Oookay. Well, I'll see ya later, Jace-face. Nice to meet you, Gregg with three 'G's.'"

Gregg edged up alongside Jacie as they headed to the west tower.

He kept silent but walked so close, Jacie thought if she stopped too fast he might run into her.

"Long day, huh?" she said, hoping to spark something, *anything* from him.

"Well, it wasn't like when I went rock climbing with my uncle, but it was long all right." Gregg hooked his thumb into his jeans pocket and began to swagger.

Oh, please, don't try to act cool.

Gregg continued, "Yeah, we were stuck up on Mount Clifford in a thunderstorm." His face grew serious. "I could have died. The elements during a storm are very dangerous."

"Mmmm." Jacie changed her mind. She didn't want *anything* from him.

"We ran short on rope and lost some of our carabiners—that's what you use to climb with. You probably didn't know that."

Oh, she wanted to say. *You mean an oblong metal ring with a spring hinge for holding a free-running rope? I'm from Colorado, remember?* Instead she said, "That sounds scary."

She felt sorry for him. He obviously needed friends. *If nothing else, I can be a friend.*

Kids moved toward the elevator, then one by one moved away. "Can you believe it?" a girl announced, motioning toward a piece of paper taped to the metal doors. "The elevators are both broken!"

"This is crazy!" said a guy dragging the heavy metal case that housed one of the portable sound systems. "How am I supposed to lug this thing up five flights of stairs?"

Jacie looked at the signs on the closed elevator doors and then at the stairs. "Consider yourself lucky," she muttered. "I have to climb up 18 floors."

Gregg tried to pry the metal doors apart. "I guess we're walking," he said. "Too bad the doors are closed. If not, I could probably shimmy up the shaft. It wouldn't be hard to go up 21 floors."

Jacie didn't know whether to scream in frustration or burst out laughing, so she just nodded and began ascending the steps. Gregg, of course, stayed close to her side.

As Jacie listened to Gregg talk about his run-in with a grizzly bear, the details of his huge aquarium, and why he thought comic books should be studied in English class instead of novels, she silently counted steps. Two hundred and fifty-two steps later, they reached Jacie's door.

Gregg finally paused.

"Where are you from, anyway?" Jacie asked, half expecting some goofy reply about a distant planet.

"Sandusky, Ohio. Y'know, where Cedar Point is."

Jacie had never heard of it, but she didn't care for a description of it either. "Ah!" she smiled. "Of course." She placed her hand on the door-knob to her room. Her friends' voices filtered through the door. "Well, I should go. I need to change—"

"No, don't change!" he screamed, sounding horrified. "I like you just the way you are!"

"Well, I'll see you," Jacie said flatly, closing the door on Gregg's guffawing laughter.

"Did you think I was serious?" he continued. "What a riot! Don't change . . ."

She rolled her eyes and shook her head in exasperation at the girls congregated in the living area.

"Where were you?" asked April. Perspiration dotted her reddened face. "You disappeared."

"Gregg helped me take the empty water bottles to the dining hall—"

Amused glances passed among the girls.

"I'll just bet that boy enjoyed his chore," Laurilee said. She sat cross-legged on the couch, her blonde braid slung over one shoulder.

"I think he's lonely," Jacie said.

"He's lonely without you," Morgan filed her nails at the dining room table. "He's been panting after you all day."

"As the deer pants for the water, so Gregg pants for Jacie," said Celia. "That's okay, you can have him. I have my sights on Corey." She leaned back on the couch and sighed.

"Where's Lia?" Jacie asked.

"Napping in her dad's room until dinnertime."

Something sad shot through Jacie.

"For about two seconds I thought how fun it would be to have my dad on our team," said Nichole. "But then I knew he'd be overprotective and drive me crazy."

"I miss my dad," said Mercedes.

"I'd be working harder if my dad were here," laughed Phoebe. "He'd make sure of that!"

Jacie couldn't even picture what her dad would do with 30 kids. He'd never felt comfortable with humans under 20, herself included. One Christmas, he gave her a briefcase. Sure, it was top-of-the-line quality, but still, a *briefcase?* His wife, Felicia, tried to cover up the faux pas by shoving gift boxes containing the latest fashions at Jacie.

Later, Felicia pulled her aside. "Jacie. Your father loves you very much. He just . . . doesn't really know what to *do* with you."

Jacie didn't want her stepmom to make excuses for him. "I like the briefcase," she insisted. "I'll carry my art supplies in it." But, of course, she never did.

● ● ●

"I think they're trying to kill us," Kylie said, inspecting the food in her hand.

"I think it's supposed to be a hamburger," Valerie said.

Jacie inspected her "burger." She bit. She chewed. She swallowed. She looked again at the object in her hand. It looked a little like a hamburger, smelled a little like a hamburger—but tasted nothing like a hamburger.

"Do you think it's dog meat?" Celia's eyes widened.

Laurilee dropped her burger.

"Don't they eat dog in Korea?" asked Nichole. "Valerie, you'd know."

Valerie rolled her almond-shaped eyes. "Yeah, in my family it's poodle or Doberman."

"Well, we are on a missions trip . . ." Joelle shrugged. She held out her burger to the middle of the table.

The other girls followed suit. "To McDonald's!"

● ● ●

"Tyler!" Jacie stood on top of a molded plastic chair and waved wildly.

"Hey, Jace!" Tyler rushed through the gathering crowd, picked her up off the chair, and spun her around. "How was your day?"

A spot of mustard clung to his cheek, and she wiped it off without thinking. "Hot, dirty, hard, and wonderful! We dug out classrooms at a flooded school. You should have seen these kids, Tyler. They were precious! Where did you go?"

"Somewhere in the middle of the city. Cement, smog, and sweat. But hey," he said, shrugging his shoulders, "we had our first performance." He puffed out his chest and imitated Vin Diesel. "I'm a prince, you know. I get to wear a cape."

"Well, I'm a clown, and I get to wear a red bulbous nose," Jacie smiled. "Our first performance is tomorrow."

"Oh . . . you'll love it. It reminds me why I'm excited about being a musician. The crowd gathering, watching, listening. I'm telling you, God can really use people who have gifts in the arts."

"Did you get to pray with anyone?" Jacie almost hated to ask. Her palms sweat at the thought of having to do it.

Tyler's head bobbed up and down. "People were *lining up* to accept

Christ. Can you imagine, Jacie? You'd never see that in the States. Men, women, kids. It rocked!"

"That's awesome. I just hope I don't scare everyone away with my big ruffled butt."

"Aw, c'mon, Jace. You look awesome in that costume," Corey said behind her. "Who could be scared of you?"

Jacie's cheeks grew warm.

"I'm Tyler Jennings." Tyler stuck out his hand. "I'm a friend of Jacie's from Colorado."

"Corey Baxter," Corey replied, returning the handshake. "I'm a friend of Jacie's from Team 10." He turned to Jacie. "We're all sitting up by the stage. We saved you a seat."

Jacie wanted to sit with Becca and Tyler but thought it would be rude to decline Corey's offer. "Thanks. I'll be up in a minute."

Corey disappeared into the jabbering crowd of teens.

"Well," Tyler said, watching him go. "He certainly has a thing for you."

"What? He's just being friendly."

"He said, 'You look awesome,' Jacie. 'Cute' and 'sweet' might be friendly. 'Awesome' means he has a thing for you. Be careful."

Jacie rolled her eyes. "Whatever."

"Well, you'd better be careful about sending those signals, then."

"What signals?"

"C'mon, Jace. You know that smile of yours is a guy magnet. Guys think, 'She likes me! Yes!' " Tyler did an impression of a football player's victory dance.

Jacie laughed. "You know I'm just being friendly. I treat everyone the same—boys, girls, dogs, cats, and old ladies."

"Ah, yes, but those poor boys don't know that. I'm telling you, Jacie Noland, you and your smile are dangerous weapons." He put his arm around her and whispered conspiratorially. "Let me tell you some top secret guy info. You think you're being friendly, but guys are interpreting that as being interested."

Jacie matched Tyler's hushed voice. "I'll try to control myself." She grinned at him then said, "Oh, was I smiling again? I'm sorry." She slapped her hand across her mouth. "Are you going to start following me? Are you going to plan our wedding? Are you going to tattoo my name on your arm? Please! No!"

Tyler punched her arm. "Okay, Ms. Melodrama Queen. Someday you'll appreciate me looking out for you."

Jacie gave him a quick hug. "I already do."

● ● ●

Jacie found the team and stood between Phoebe and April. Phoebe welcomed her with an arm-around-the-shoulder squeeze. "This is my favorite part of the day. Mega-awesome," she said as the electric guitar on stage began the opening chords.

"Me, too," Jacie responded. "It's when I can feel God's presence."

Phoebe nodded, understanding. "Exactly."

God, thanks for such a great day . . . and for putting me on such a great team.

Jacie closed her eyes and let the words and music fill her.

I could sing of Your love forever . . .

Jacie, believing the words with her whole heart, raised her face, reached up her arms . . . She thought she could almost see God on His throne—

" 'Scuse me, 'scuse me," a loud voice broke in. A body pushed between Jacie and Phoebe.

"Jacie," Gregg said, not even trying to keep his voice down. "I didn't see you come in. I waited by the door."

"Well, here I am," she whispered back, keeping her eyes closed.

"I brought pictures of me rock climbing since you were so interested and all." He grabbed an arm and thrust the pile of photos into her hand.

"You can look at them now since we're only singing and stuff."

• • •

"Hold still!" April insisted.

"But it tickles," Jacie said. She bit the inside of her cheek, to remain motionless while April finished applying the clown makeup.

"Done." April leaned back and examined Jacie's face. "And done well if I do say so myself."

"Thanks. I'll be the clown of the ball."

"Let's go!" Melanie said. She always seemed to appear and disappear without any warning. Today she looked like an odd combination of cheerleader and traffic cop getting the team on the bus. "Let's go, let's go, Team 10! You ROCK. You are going to turn Caracas upside down!" She bounced with excitement.

"Well," April whispered to Jacie, "guess someone's feeling better today."

Jacie snickered and nodded.

Armed with props and dressed in their costumes, the kids boarded the bus.

"You are the perfect clown," Berk said, sitting in the front seat. "The dimples make it."

"Really?" Jacie asked, her heart warming at his praise. "I'm so nervous. I don't feel much like a clown." She looked down at her lap, hoping he didn't see the longing for a father like him in her eyes.

"You'll be fine," Berk assured her. "You'll get out there and smile and waggle-walk, and everyone will love you."

Jacie took a deep breath. "I hope so." She turned to look out the window, wiping her damp hands for the fifth time down the silky green stripe on her costume. No one else seemed to be nervous. They all chattered and laughed and threw things.

Jacie held her breath as the bus turned sharp corners onto smaller streets. Parked cars lined the narrow streets, leaving only inches for the bus to pass. Multicolored one-room shanties stair-stepped up the hillside. Jacie tilted her head to see these crumbling homes. *God*, she whispered, *I'll never complain about our little townhouse again.*

Exhaust poured into the open windows. Jacie felt sticky and wet inside her costume. She'd taken a shower in the morning, but the dirty air hung so heavy, she felt she needed another one. Even so, gratitude flowed through her for the life she had in the States.

The bus finally turned a corner and squealed to a halt in front of a busy park—much like the one the day before. There were the same crowds of men, smoking cigarettes and just hanging around.

"Gather 'round!" Melanie called. "Prayer time. Laurilee. Pray for our performance to be honoring to God, and pray for the audience."

"Yes, Miss Melanie," Laurilee drawled. She prayed a sweet prayer, touching Jacie deeply.

But the moment Laurilee spoke the "amen," Jacie felt a surge of fear. Hannah grabbed her hand. "Let's go," she said softly. Jacie smiled, knowing Hannah didn't like being the center of attention any more than she did. In this, they were exactly alike. They could stick together.

By the time the guys had set up the sound system, a curious crowd had formed around the silly-looking group.

The music swelled from the portable sound system, calling a hundred kids who swarmed down the hill to the park. All of them wore navy blue shorts or skirts and once-crisp white shirts—the national school uniform for the third grade.

Corey shot her an excited grin. Phoebe's face glowed. Hannah stood, eyes closed, mouth barely moving in a silent prayer. Jacie could feel her stomach knotting. They'd practiced over and over again, but she suddenly wished they'd rehearsed it more. She knew she'd forget her cues or turn the wrong way. *At least there aren't any lines to remember.*

"Nervous?" whispered Lia.

"That's an understatement."

"Well, you know they say that when you get nervous in front of a crowd, you're supposed to picture them in their underwear."

Jacie looked up at the nearest audience member. An old man with gray chest hair bursting from his shirt and a plump belly that hung over his belt smiled at Jacie, wiggling his eyebrows flirtatiously.

She turned back to Lia. "I don't think that's such a good idea."

● ● ●

The performance had glitches only the cast members would notice. Afterwards, Berk caught a giggling Lia up in his arms before sending her off into the swarming crowd to talk to those interested in what the drama meant to them. Jacie wanted him to scoop her up and tell her what a great job she'd done. Instead, she turned her attention to the mound of backpacks she'd volunteered to watch. What would she actually do if someone came up and grabbed one? Chase them down and tackle them?

It didn't matter. Standing there staring at backpacks beat wandering through the crowd with a witnessing cue card in English and Spanish. She plopped to the ground, watching the rest of her team spread through the crowd. They read from their cue cards while groups of people stood, listening intently.

They make it look so easy.

An older woman prayed with an interpreter. A group of three little girls listened intently as Phoebe spoke and waved her arms for emphasis. Two teen guys laughed with Corey and Berk.

And here I sit. I guess I could pray.

Lia plunked down heavily next to her. "Wasn't that awesome? Did you see how many people came forward?"

Jacie nodded. "Yeah. Even with a clumsy clown." She reached for her water to squelch a tickling in her throat.

"You were perfect." Lia patted Jacie's knee. "You made the show." She paused. "Do you know what's wrong with Hannah? She seems really upset."

"She does?" Jacie searched the crowd for her.

"Yeah. She went to the bus a minute ago."

"That's weird," Jacie said. "Hannah would *never* walk away from a chance to share the gospel."

"Well, she didn't walk away from this one. She *ran*."

chapter 9

God, this morning I was so excited about the chance to share YOU with people after the performance. I practiced the gospel questions in Spanish a hundred times. But when I talked to three Venezuelans just now, they just stared at me. I might as well have been speaking gibberish. Nichole came along with the same card, asked the same questions, and they responded. They asked to accept Christ! I should be happy. I should be rejoicing. But I'm frustrated. Why didn't You use ME?

If Aunt Dinah was here, she'd know what went wrong. She's traveled all over *the world. People have always responded to her charming laugh and animated personality.*

Hannah chewed on the end of her pen. Only a couple of months ago, Aunt Dinah stood at the front of the church in her wedding dress, exchanging vows. Hannah stood there with her as the maid of honor. At the reception, despite the flurry of photos and toasts, Aunt Dinah had remembered—

"So? What about Venezuela?"

"I'm going!" Hannah squealed. "The letter arrived yesterday!"

Aunt Dinah threw her arms around Hannah. "I'm so excited for you! I promise I'll be your biggest prayer warrior. But you have to promise me something too."

"What?"

"Just be who God wants you to be. Nothing more, nothing less."

"Of course!" Hannah agreed, already knowing exactly what that was. *An evangelist.*

Hannah watched as her excited teammates began to fill the bus. This morning, had she allowed herself to be less? Should she have tried one more time before giving up and running like a coward to the bus? She pressed her lips into a firm line.

Next time I won't quit.

● ● ●

The bus doors opened with a hiss.

"Okay, everyone, get your things together. We need to hurry," Melanie called from the front seat. Her police arm waved in circles, attempting to get them to move faster. Hannah grabbed her prop—a tiara—and joined the throng leaving the bus. They circled around a makeshift stage against what appeared to be the outer wall of a prison. Inmates squeezed their faces between the bars, their cheeks squished tight against them. They called, shouted, and whistled at the girls, waving their arms.

Hannah felt suddenly conscious of being female. She wrapped her arms around herself and looked at the ground.

A voice called to her, "*Hola, chica. Muy, muy bonita, sí?*"

"*Sí, sí,*" several other voices called in agreement.

Hannah turned away as her face flushed with more than just the heat of embarrassment. It was seriously hot. She tried to find something to distract herself from the continued calls from behind the bars. *This would be a great time for a pep talk,* thought Hannah, noticing that the jubilant energy that had filled Team 10 after the last performance was beginning to wane.

She dug through her backpack to find her Bible, racking her brain for the perfect verse to encourage her teammates. *Maybe something from Philippians . . .*

"It's so hot I think I'm going to pass out," Kylie announced.

"And I'm out of water," chimed Valerie.

Joelle tossed a water bottle to her. "Don't you see? Hot, discouraged, and tired is right where the Enemy wants us. And you know what that means?"

"That he's doing a good job?" suggested Kylie.

"No! That we're doing something right! We should look at this situation with God's eyes. God must be preparing people's hearts to hear the gospel. Otherwise, the Enemy wouldn't be trying so hard to discourage us."

Joelle's excitement was contagious.

"Joelle's right," said Nichole. "We need to be praising God for what He's about to do, not complaining about things."

Hannah thumbed through her Bible, trying to catch the wave of renewed enthusiasm. "And it says in Philippians, chapter four—"

"Hannah," Berk broke in, "maybe you could share that later. We need to perform ASAP. Let's get into our places, gang." The group dispersed, pumped with excitement.

"Thanks, Joelle." Berk tweaked the brunette's hair. "Well said."

Hannah pursed her lips. *I will not act childish just because Joelle beat me to it.*

Hannah gathered with her prayer group as they passionately asked God to break down barriers in people's hearts and keep distractions at bay so that He could make the message clear.

Now Hannah felt anticipation pumping through her veins. *This is it. God has placed people in that crowd that I'm going to pray with to accept Christ.* When they finished, she saw the crowd had almost doubled in size. While several dozen inmates watched through barred windows on one side, a large crowd of people gathered on the other, packed like sardines around the stage. Children climbed on top of a nearby fence, and mothers held toddlers on their shoulders so they could see. *There must be 300 people here*, she thought. Hannah contained her excitement by snapping a few quick shots before tucking her camera in her backpack.

Joelle played with the red scarf tied around her waist. "Can you believe it?" she grabbed Hannah's hand. "Melanie asked me to give the invitation. Will you pray for me while I'm doing it? I really want God to use me."

Why didn't Melanie ask me? Hannah forced a smile. "Of course I will."

"*Bienvenidos*," the interpreter said into the microphone.

Joelle squeezed Hannah's hand. "Break a leg," she whispered.

● ● ●

Hannah poured her heart into the performance, making it her best yet. She was more graceful and expressive, and her timing was perfect. But it seemed like everything she did was funny because the audience laughed whenever she was on stage.

As the music faded, the group lined up to bow. Joelle took the microphone and, after the applause died down, she shared the gospel message. She invited anyone who wanted to accept Christ to come up to the stage. Immediately, people from all directions flooded forward.

"Okay, Team 10, go talk to someone," said Berk. The teens moved out into the crowd.

"Hannah," Melanie called, "could you please watch the bags?"

Hannah drew her brows together, surprised. *What about Jacie?* But Jacie stood behind Melanie, nodding in agreement.

"I was hoping to go talk to them." Hannah pointed at a cluster of women. "They looked interested."

"I need you to watch the bags," Melanie said. "And I want to tie this around your waist." She thrust a sweatshirt into Hannah's hands.

"Why?"

Melanie pulled her over against a wall near the pile of bags. A group of guys walked by, looked at Hannah, and laughed.

"Hannah," Melanie said in a hushed voice, "do you remember while we were in Miami Dr. Rick told us that traveling could cause our cycles to—" she paused, searching for the right word, "—to surprise us?"

"Yeah, he said—" Hannah stopped short. She felt her face go ashen. "Melanie, did . . . ?"

"Yes, I'm sorry, Hannah. We'll find you a bathroom as soon as we can."

"You mean, every time . . . ?" Hannah replayed her entire performance, remembering the laughter, the jeering faces, the pointing. Of course! How could she not have realized it before? "They were laughing at me."

Melanie gestured toward the huge crowd. "Look how God used the drama anyway." She gave her a hug. "Don't worry. You didn't spoil God working in the hearts of people."

Hannah was horrified.

Melanie put her arm around her. "I know it's not much comfort, but look at it this way: At least you'll never see these people again."

Hannah nodded, but humiliation overwhelmed her.

● ● ●

That night when the opening worship song began, Hannah closed her eyes. The moment she did, she saw mocking, pointing inmates. She opened her eyes and stared up into the sky. Clouds highlighted by the setting sun became blotches on her dress. She sang louder to chase away the memory. It didn't work. She gave up singing and watched her teammates. They seemed to be worshipping in the presence of God. But Hannah couldn't feel it.

And step by step You'll lead me . . .

Her mouth formed the words, but her heart felt miles away.

Worship dragged on and on, then Redman performed his wacky stunts on stage. Numbness consumed Hannah. She watched dully as Susie Shellenberger, sporting another Coca-Cola pajama pants set, took her place in front.

"Before I get into the Word tonight," Susie began, "I'd like to hear about your day. Did God do something or what?"

The entire room cheered—except for Hannah.

Susie continued, "I'd like to get a few volunteers up here to tell us what God did in your team." She scanned the audience, selecting a few teens from the sea of raised hands. Joelle was one of the first up front.

"Hi! My name is Joelle Birchwood and I'm from Team 10." Shouts and cheers burst from all over the room.

"Go, Joelle!" one of the guys shouted.

"We had an awesome day! At our first performance 50 people came to know the Lord. Almost all of our team members had the opportunity to lead someone to Christ, some of us for the first time. God really gave us the wisdom and words to share. It *so* wasn't us."

It wasn't me, either.

"That's great!" Susie commented.

croutons for breakfast

Yeah. Terrific.

"At our second performance, it seemed like the Enemy was working overtime to get us discouraged. We were so hot and tired when we set up that we felt like the Israelites in the desert."

Joelle scrunched up her face and the crowd laughed. She continued. "But we knew God could use us no matter what."

"So what happened?" asked Susie.

Everyone laughed at me. That's what happened.

"Well," Joelle allowed for a dramatic pause. "One hundred and thirty people came forward to accept Christ! Praise God!"

The room exploded with shouts and cheers. Team 10 was on their feet. Hannah felt she'd better stand up too.

● ● ●

As the girls got ready for bed that night, they resembled a team that had just won a state championship .

Lia stood on the kitchen table singing show tunes into a hairbrush.

Jill danced around the living room in her newly created toilet paper wedding dress.

Mercedes and Valerie set up a limbo stick.

Hannah sneaked into the bathroom and locked the door behind her.

Joelle knocked on the bathroom door. "Hannah, come out here. We're having so much fun."

"I'm sorry, Joelle. I think I'm going to go straight to bed."

"Are you feeling okay?" Joelle's muffled voice sounded genuinely concerned. "Do you need anything?"

"No. Thanks, though."

Hannah crawled into bed a few minutes later. She lay there with her eyes wide open, not tired at all, hearing muted chatter and giggles through the closed door. *One hundred and eighty people asked Christ into their hearts today, and I didn't pray with a single one.* A tear rolled down her cheek and Hannah hurriedly brushed it away. She rolled over and switched on the light. She found her journal and began to pour out her heart to God.

> *God, I should be praising You for all that You did today. 180 people! Wow! But I'm not, and I feel terrible about it. Why didn't You use me, God? I so much want to lead people to You. You know that. And evangelism is obviously my gift—I told You I'm ready to serve. Do I have unconfessed sin? If I do, please reveal it to me now.*

Hannah squeezed her eyes shut and waited. Nothing. She sighed and opened her eyes.

Fine. Just forgive me for whatever. She sighed. *What a bad attitude! This is probably the most awful day of my life, and it was supposed to be one of the best. But tomorrow will be better, right?*

chapter 10

The next day, as the group was getting off the bus, Kylie grumbled, "Great. Look who's here."

Jacie glanced past her. Jared, the missionary's son who had been so mean, leaned against a signpost, looking as sullen as ever. He wore a white tank top that showed off his well-toned muscles, and Jacie thought that without the icy stare, he might have been kind of cute.

"If he doesn't want to be here, he should just stay at home," Kylie added, voicing Jacie's other thought.

But even more than all that, Jacie was curious. What made him so angry? Maybe he just resented being the son of a missionary. She decided to try to be more understanding.

Hank spoke to his son, squeezing his shoulder before turning to greet the group. The vulnerable look that crossed Jared's face just before Hank turned grabbed Jacie's heart, and suddenly she ached for him.

"Great to see you all again!" Hank boomed. "Today we're going to be carrying bricks to rebuild the church up on this hill."

Jacie looked to where he pointed. Up the mountain, the crumbling foundation of a church sat halfway up a long flight of narrow steps, among thousands of hillside shanties. A rough, decaying wooden cross stood next to it.

"Jared will take half of you up to the church, and the rest of us will work down here," Hank explained.

Melanie counted Team 10 off by twos. Jacie found herself in Jared's group. She trudged up as part of the single file line behind him, careful not to lose her footing on the crumbling stone steps. *We're supposed to carry bricks up these?* "Bummer. We would have to get stuck with Eeyore," Kylie whispered to Jacie.

"I feel bad for him," Jacie said.

Kylie shrugged. "I don't. But I do feel bad for anyone he's supposed to be ministering to."

When they finally reached the top of the stairs, Jared tartly explained where they would clear spaces for the bricks to be stacked. Up close, Jacie noticed his tan face accentuated his clear, steel blue eyes.

"Who is going to finish this church?" asked Corey. "This looks impossible."

Jared folded his arms across his chest. "How 'bout you just do what I'm asking and don't worry about the rest?"

Corey straightened and met his eyes.

Jared didn't flinch. Instead, he continued, "We need this foundation cleared by lunchtime. Let's get to work."

The group worked hard all morning with barely a word spoken among them. When lunchtime was announced, it was Corey who was first to break the code of silence.

"Could someone grab me a sandwich?" he asked, stacking another brick on the pile.

"Me, too!" added Jill.

"I will," Jacie volunteered.

"While you're over there, could you stick my hat in my backpack?" Mercedes asked.

"Mine, too?" Kylie called from the other side of the church.

Within moments, Jacie had agreed to run errands for virtually everyone in the group.

As she climbed out of the foundation, laden with cameras, T-shirts, hats, trash, and Hannah's sunscreen, Jacie sang a song to remind herself of all the things she was going for. "Hi, ho. Hi, ho. It's off for food I go. I'll grab a snack and put a hat in the green backpack, and then I'll stuff a shirt—" Her singing faltered as she realized Jared was watching her.

Jacie smiled and waved with her only free appendage—her left foot. "How's it going, Jared?" The awkward movement was enough to shift her balance, and she dropped the hat. Trying to grab it, she let a T-shirt slip out of her hand, along with a camera. The entire load collapsed in a clumsy pile at her feet. "Oops."

Jared shook his head and turned away.

Fine, Mr. Sourpuss. If you hate being here so much, why don't you just leave?

After Jacie had completed her errands, she sought out the sandwiches. Hank sat near the sandwich makers, engaging them in jovial conversation.

"Excuse me, Hank," Jacie said. "I'm sorry to interrupt you. But I wondered if Jared likes PB&J."

Hank nodded. "Indeed he does, Madam."

"Good!" Jacie loaded up stacks of the gooey filled rolls into her arms. "Jacie. I don't think he needs that many," Hank teased.

"You kidding?" She winked. "These are for me."

Hank put his hand on Jacie's shoulder. "Jared's a little rough around the edges, but he's a good kid. Thanks for being patient with him."

"I brought you a couple sandwiches, Jared." Jacie held out two torpedo rolls.

Jared stacked bricks without stopping. He didn't even look at her. "No, thanks."

"C'mon. Peanut butter is protein and jelly is . . . well . . . sugar."

"I'm not hungry."

Jacie sighed. "I'll leave them here for you in case you change your mind."

Jared paused to look at her, stone-faced, then went back to stacking his bricks.

Berk arrived, his face wet with perspiration from the steep climb. "Hey, everyone, here's some news to get you through the day," he announced. "We're heading to McDonald's when we're done."

Whoops and cheers erupted from the group. Jacie wasn't a huge fan of McDonald's—or hamburgers in general—but anything "normal" sounded pretty good at this point.

"Maybe that will erase the memory of those pseudo-burgers we had a couple nights ago," Morgan said.

"Uh, before you go, I could use a little help over here," Jared growled, interrupting the happy clamor. Jacie could tell he hated asking for it, but it would obviously take two people to carry the long boards he was trying to move.

No one volunteered.

Jacie spoke up. "I'll help you."

He brusquely explained what needed to be done, and Jacie set to helping him in silence. Occasionally, she asked a question, mostly just trying to get him to say something, but Jared barely responded.

"You like living in Venezuela?"

"It's okay."

"Your dad seems really cool."

"He's all right."

"How long do you think you'll stay?"

Shrug.

"Do you think—"

"Listen, Marisa, you don't have to put on the happy-snappy-small-talk thing. I'm just—"

"Jacie," she corrected through clenched teeth.

"What?"

"My name is Jacie."

He stared back. *Steel blue. Like sapphires.*

"Jared, could you tell me where I can find a restroom?" Hannah approached them, looking like she was about ready to explode.

"Yeah," Jacie echoed, wiping a stream of sweat trickling down her face. "I could use one too."

Jared looked annoyed. "Couldn't you wait a couple hours?"

"No," both girls said in unison.

He muttered something and pointed toward the street below. "Bottom of the steps. Grocery store around the corner should let you use theirs."

"Well, how about that? The Nazi-missionary will let us go to the bathroom," Hannah mumbled as they navigated their way down the steps.

"Hannah!" Jacie's jaw about dropped off. "You sound like Solana!"

"Oops."

Jacie laughed. "Don't worry. I love it!"

The girls found Hank and explained their plight.

"That's fine," Hank said. Jacie noticed his sun-reddened cheeks made him look even more like Santa Claus. "I've already talked to the manager. It's right around the corner. But stay together."

The girls followed the direction of his finger to *La Groceria Verde*. Two large men in baseball caps argued near the entrance. A roly-poly man behind the counter barely looked up as he nodded in the direction of the bathroom. Jacie had already become accustomed to the grimy public restrooms in the parks and had armed herself with antibacterial gel.

While they figured out how to flush by pouring a bucket of water into the commode, Hannah snickered. "Boy, this makes me appreciate the toilets at the hotel," she said. "At least we can flush those."

"Once a day," Jacie said wryly. "We should hurry, though. We don't want Jared on our case."

Jacie opened the door and found herself staring straight into a large man's chest. She could smell cigarette smoke and booze clinging to him. He clutched a brown bag in his greasy fist.

"Excuse us," she said, trying to move past him.

The man stood still. Jacie stepped to the side. The man mirrored her. The man behind him said something in Spanish, and they both laughed.

Jacie turned to look at Hannah, noticing her face had paled and her blue eyes widened. The shopkeeper was nowhere to be seen.

Suddenly, the man grabbed Jacie's wrist, and she looked up at his scowling face. Cigarette ashes clung to his beard, and several teeth were twisted out of place.

"Venga, chica."

"No!" Jacie tried to pull her wrist away, but the man gripped it tighter. Horror scenes flashed through Jacie's mind. Her helplessness in the situation hit her like a rock in the stomach. She saw the smirk of the second man, the hairy hand clenching her wrist, the twisted, snarled teeth.

"Let go of her!" Berk's strong voice came up behind the men.

The men turned, startled.

"Leave!" Fire shot from Berk's eyes as he pointed insistently to the door. "Now!"

The men looked at each other, muttered more Spanish, and left.

Gentleness washed over Berk's hardened face as he turned to the girls. "Are you okay?"

Jacie nodded.

"Now we are. Thanks," Hannah said.

"How'd you know we were in trouble?" Jacie asked.

"I didn't want you to be here by yourself, so I was on my way into the store. I'm sorry I wasn't standing guard from the beginning," he said.

"We're just so glad you came at all," Hannah said.

Although the interaction with the two men had probably only lasted 30 seconds, it was just enough time to scare the girls half to death.

As they left the store, Hannah said something about "the world we live in," but Jacie barely heard it.

"Are you sure you're all right, Jacie?" Berk placed his hand on Jacie's shoulder. "Do you want to sit down?"

It was only then she noticed her heart racing. Time seemed to have stopped and picked up again, the terror and panic rushing back to the surface. She couldn't allow herself to imagine what might have happened if Berk hadn't stepped in.

"I'm . . . I'm glad you were here," her thin voice squeaked.

Berk squatted down on his heels and looked up at Jacie. His eyes became serious and he spoke slowly. "Of course I was here. I'm not going to let anything hurt you, you understand? I'm here to protect you."

Jacie nodded as tears begin spilling out of her eyes and down her cheeks. Berk pulled her close to him in a warm daddy hug. Jacie sobbed, feeling Berk's strong hand patting her back. "It's okay, Jacie."

Jacie suddenly pulled back, wiping the tears away with the back of her hand. "I'm fine."

"Are you sure?"

Jacie nodded. "Yeah." She looked around. "We should probably get back to work."

"Only if you're up to it," Berk said.

Jacie nodded, and a smile emerged. "You bet."

Hannah began talking a mile a minute. "I'm sure they were drinking. I could smell it on the older guy's breath. And the younger one looked dazed too. Do you think they were on drugs? Do they have drugs here?"

Berk walked silently between the two girls the short distance back to the work site. Jacie found herself watching the Venezuelan men more closely. But she wasn't scared. As long as she walked next to Berk, no one would bother her.

● ● ●

The remainder of the afternoon passed in slow, super-heated motion. The intense, relentless sun and sticky humidity slowed the teens to a sluggish pace. The dust seemed to be settling into Jacie's throat and lungs. She poured water in, but nothing seemed to take away that annoying tickle.

Jared shook his head in disgust. "We'll never finish by the end of the day. Everyone's gone into 'slacker mode.' I thought you came on this trip to work."

"It's HOT," someone yelled in defense.

Jacie took off her hat and wiped her forehead with it. "Give us a chance, Jared. I think we can do it."

Several Team 10 members murmured at Jacie's unrealistic optimism.

Jared gave her a quick look, then continued to dig.

Jacie put her hands on her hips. "Jared, I'll make a deal with you." Jared's head jerked up.

"We'll be done by four."

"What?" Kylie's mouth dropped open. "Don't promise him that, Jacie!"

"There's no way," Jared said, stone-faced. "You slackers couldn't finish if you worked until five. And your bus leaves at four."

Leaning on his shovel, Corey asked, "You don't think we can work? What do you think we've been doing?"

Jared's expression of stone turned toward Corey. "I don't think you can do what they've assigned us to do by four. You've been slacking."

"You don't think we can do this?" Hannah asked, her arm sweeping out to indicate the piles still left to be moved.

By now the group had circled around Jared, waiting for his response.

"Honestly? No."

"What if we prove you wrong?"

Jared looked around the group. He shook his head.

Jacie spoke up. "If we prove you wrong, you'll have to eat an ice cream—"

"Topped with French fries—" called Gregg.

"And ketchup!" added April.

"—at McDonald's."

Jared shrugged. "Fine. Whatever. It's not like you're going to do it anyway."

"C'mon, Team 10," Corey yelled, grabbing an armload of bricks. "You heard the man. Let's shoot for double-turbo mode."

A cool wind breezed through and snapped the faces to life. Suddenly, everyone scattered to their different tasks.

Jacie stood there amazed, watching the reenergized group work with new vitality. Jared just stared.

Jacie gave Jared a stern look. "Hey. You're not off the hook either, Mister. You still have to do your part. So get to it!"

Jared muttered something under his breath and turned back to work.

But something was different. *Was that a smile on his face?* Jacie looked closer. *Yes, definitely the beginning of a smile.*

● ● ●

Jacie plunked down on one of McDonald's familiar swivel seats. Some things were the same no matter where you were—God, friends, and McDonald's. And there was nothing Jacie wanted more after all the croutons, peanut butter and jelly, and pseudo-burgers, than a Quarter Pounder with cheese and fries. *Mmm . . . heavenly.* She munched blissfully on her hamburger, not even noticing when Corey and Jared took the seats next to her. They'd seemed to hit it off after sitting together on the bus.

"Someone's enjoying herself," Corey noted.

Kylie sat across from him. "It tastes like America," she said through a mouthful.

"Y'know, you are in America—only South America instead of North," said Jared. It was still sarcastic, but the edge in his tone had softened.

"Whatever," Kylie said.

Corey nabbed Jacie's bag of fries and passed them behind her back. "Hey, Jared. Up for a game of keep-away?"

"Maybe."

"Hey!" Jacie whined. "Salt and grease are my lifeblood!"

Jared held the pouch of fries over Jacie's head, just out of reach of her short frame. She jumped up and down, but he kept moving them upwards.

"Fine," she said. "I'll just eat my hambur— Hey!" Her burger had been swiped.

Corey held it behind his back and swiveled his chair to avoid Jacie's reach.

"Fries, Jacie?" Jared lowered the still-steaming pouch under her nose then snatched them away.

She jumped for them again but caught air.

"It's the Jacie Noland workout program," Corey announced in his best John Madden voice. "Today it's a tough series of fat-burning conditioning exercises. Just look at those jumps and reaches!"

The rest of the team rolled with laughter. Realizing how silly she looked, Jacie laughed too.

Jared took over the play-by-play. "We'll make her work to the end, folks. One more set of fry jumps . . ."

"And hamburger reaches. One . . . two . . . three . . . four," Corey counted, swiveling right and left.

Jacie laughed until she was out of breath.

"Rewards for a good training session," said Jared as he set the fries in front of her, nabbing one for himself.

"I never knew fast food could burn so many calories," Joelle commented.

"I never knew Jared could be so fun," Jacie added. She slapped her hand over her mouth. "I mean . . . I didn't mean . . ."

"Uh-huh. Whatever, fry-gal."

The table fell silent, and Jacie chided herself. *I'm such an idiot.*

"Boy, Jacie," Gregg exclaimed loud enough for everyone in the restaurant to hear. "You can flirt and put your foot in your mouth at the same time."

Thanks, Gregg. Tyler's words came back to her mind. *You think you're being friendly, but guys think you're interested.*

Hannah arrived, slipping a melting bowl of ice cream in front of Jared. "It's time, buddy," she said.

Jacie donated the remainder of her fries, and Gregg doused the sundae with three packets of ketchup.

Team 10 crowded around the table.

"Okay, Jared. You lost! You eat!" Jacie announced. She grabbed her soda and took a quick swig, the annoying tickle growing stronger in her throat and chest.

Jared sighed. "I hoped you'd forget."

"As if!" Nichole shouted. "Eat!"

"EAT, EAT, EAT, EAT," the crowd chanted.

Jacie linked arms with Hannah, and the two laughed through the chants.

Jared lifted the spoon. He looked at the crowd, who chanted louder. He dipped it into the gooey sundae and lifted the laden spoon to his mouth. Into his mouth went three fries, glistening ice cream, and ketchup.

"EWWW!" the girls groaned.

Jared munched, a grin spreading across his face. Then he bent to the task and snarfed the rest of the concoction without hesitation. When he finished, he wiped his mouth with a flourish. "Yum!"

"Gross!" Kylie said.

"Actually," Jared said, "there are restaurants in Pittsburgh that serve ice cream and French fries. It's really not that bad. I used to order—"

"What?" Kylie shrieked. "You've eaten this before?"

Jared shrugged. "Sure."

Stunned, disappointed silence fell over the group. And then, Jacie started to laugh. Everyone else joined her. "Why didn't you say something?" she asked.

Jared's smile grew across his face. "Because I wanted you to finish by four."

Jacie whacked his shoulder with the backside of her hand. "YOU—" but she couldn't think how to finish the sentence.

"Will you be at our next work project, Jared?" Celia asked.

"We have another one tomorrow," Berk said.

"Where?"

Berk checked the schedule in his binder. "It says *El Camanero*."

"This time we'll make sure to challenge you with something really gross," Jacie offered.

Darkness crossed Jared's face. "I need to go. I'll—"

He walked out without looking back.

Gregg watched him go. "And I thought women had mood swings . . . wow!"

Jacie felt awash in shame. Jared had started opening up, but her stupid mouth had done it again—she'd shot him right back down.

"You've been quiet tonight," Hannah said.

"I've been thinking," Jacie whispered. Her throat burned despite her repeated attempts to ignore it. She downed vitamin C drops, one after the other. "What a day."

Hannah nodded. "Isn't it sad how some of the people here live? We take so much for granted."

"Yeah," Jacie paused. "I was thinking more about how Berk rescued us today." *And how I ruined Jared's fun.*

"Rescued us?" Hannah's eyebrows shot up. "Oh, you mean at the grocery store? That seems like forever ago."

"It felt pretty good."

"It felt better than having those guys after us." Hannah shuddered.

"I'm glad he was there. He flew in like Superman or something."

"Well, that's what he's supposed to do. It's his job."

"Weren't you surprised?" Jacie asked.

Hannah scowled for a moment and then her face softened. "Not really. My dad would have done the same thing. He's like a hawk as he watches over his family."

Jacie swallowed back her tears and felt them burn on her throat.

"Sometimes, I think Dad goes a little overboard," Hannah said. "But I know it's because he loves us."

Jacie nodded. She looked at Hannah, who smiled and talked about her family's adventures. *God, Hannah always feels safe—safe and protected. Why don't I ever get to feel that way?* Jacie couldn't think of even one time when she felt completely safe. Until today. Sure, her mom cared who she went out with, but that was different. Besides, her mother wasn't that strong.

Maybe I've just grown accustomed to living in a scary world, she thought. And today was a very real glimpse of just how scary the world could be.

Hannah stretched, thankful for a new day. A new beginning. Hard work the day before had washed from her the confusion and self-loathing she had felt after the performances. She looked around the apartment. Everything was quiet with most of the girls still sleeping. She retrieved her devotional book from the bed stand and padded toward the living room, exchanging a soft "good morning" with Morgan, who sat in the hallway shaving her legs. Mercedes sat cross-legged between the dresser and the wall, reading her Bible. April stared out a window while she braided her hair. Warm sunlight filtered through the open windows, leaving long paths of light on the carpet. The air smelled of smog mixed with gardenias. The traffic noise played a constant hum in the background.

Sitting at the kitchen table, she clicked open her pen.

Thanks, God, for such a peaceful morning.

As if to contradict her, rough coughs barked from the living room. A body convulsed on the couch with each cough. Hannah grabbed a water bottle.

"Are you okay?" She stared down at the mass of tangled blankets. Jacie peered out, looking like she hadn't slept at all. She coughed and hacked, her watery eyes pleading for mercy. Hannah placed the back of her hand on Jacie's forehead.

"You're burning up, Jace."

Jacie tried to sit up but collapsed back down. "I feel awful," she croaked. Another fit of coughing shook her body, crumpling her in half.

"Drink this," Hannah said.

Jacie sucked on the water and the coughs subsided.

Lia rose up from the floor at Jacie's covered feet. Leopard-print panties peeked out from under the hem of her undersized sleep shirt. "You look awful. I'll get Melanie."

"No," Jacie groaned. "She'll make me stay here. I want to go work."

But Lia was already in the hallway, the door slamming behind her. The door reopened. "After I get dressed." Lia gave a sheepish grin and tugged on her short nightshirt to cover herself.

"Was there anyone out there?" gasped Hannah.

"Just one very startled cleaning lady." Lia winced while the other girls laughed.

Lia appeared a short time later with Melanie and a doctor. It took only a brief moment to diagnose bronchitis, sore throat, and fever. The doctor insisted Jacie stay in bed.

"It's only a work day," Melanie said over and over. "If you stay in bed, chances are you'll feel good enough tomorrow for our next performance. Besides, today we're helping out at a hospital. You don't want to spread germs, do you?"

Jacie's face crumpled. "I guess not."

While everyone else got ready, Lia and Hannah sat on the floor next to Jacie and prayed for her. When Hannah opened her eyes, she saw tears trickling down Jacie's face, puddling in her ears.

Hannah gave her a hug. "It won't be the same without you."

● ● ●

"This is a hospital?" Morgan's eyes opened wide. "In the States this place would break every code in the books."

Melanie put her finger to her lips. Even if the people milling around the cramped hallway couldn't understand her, they'd certainly pick up on her critical tone.

Hannah kept quiet, trying not to gasp as she looked around. The hospital was fairly clean, but primitive. It clearly lacked modern equipment and furnishings. Thirty or so people lined the outside porch—dirty bandages and rags wrapped around various body parts. Several children squeezed onto a bench, their feet swinging well above the worn floors.

"Welcome, welcome, *mis amigos*," boomed a deep voice through an open doorway. A round-faced, smiling gentleman in a white lab coat shook hands as he entered the room. "We are so happy you are here." Despite his heavy accent, he was easy to understand, and his smile spoke more than his words. Hannah guessed him to be about her dad's age.

"I am Dr. Manuel Servisa and the director of this hospital. I was very excited to hear you were coming."

"We're glad to be here," Melanie said, speaking for the team.

Hannah smiled. She liked Dr. Servisa immediately.

"As you will see when I give you the tour, these people desperately need encouragement and hope. And, most of all, they need Jesus."

"Are you a Christian?" Hannah blurted out the words with surprise.

The doctor smiled. "Yes. Although there is a Christian population here in Caracas, you will find that most people in the city believe in God, but do not have a personal relationship with Jesus Christ."

"Well, that's why we're here," chimed in Joelle.

"Indeed." The doctor smiled and motioned them to follow him.

"We will start out in the children's ward up those stairs on your left."

Popped paint blisters on the walls peeled onto the chipped cement steps. The team followed the doctor up the narrow stairway and paused outside a closed door.

"This is our infant ward," he announced over his shoulder. "Only a few at a time, please. There's not much room."

Hannah waited with the rest of the team in the barren hallway as a few went in. No chairs or pictures, just dingy beige walls and scuffed floors. She snapped a few photos, wanting to save film for what lay ahead. *The infant ward photos will make good pictures for my thank-you letter.*

When it came her turn, Hannah entered the tiny room, looking through the viewfinder of her camera. A dozen small cribs lined the walls, as tightly packed as the hillside shanties. Several mothers sat on shaky wooden chairs, watching the babies with worried, tired eyes. A few looked up as the group walked in. The camera dropped to Hannah's side as the enormity of the scene hit her. *If only I could take these children home with me,* she thought.

One young mother gently stroked her baby's hand with her finger. The tiny child's chest moved up and down with the effort of breathing. His face was pale. A yellowed IV tube emerged from the sole of his tiny foot.

"Oh." The word escaped like a breath. The very core of Hannah's heart seized with emotion. *Why, God, why?*

The mother turned, and the emotion in her face filled Hannah with more sadness. Despair. Agony. Hopelessness.

She reached out to touch the woman's arm, and the woman broke into sobs. Hannah hugged her as she began wailing in Spanish. Hannah listened and nodded as though she understood, stroking the young woman's thick black hair.

The rest of the hospital tour went by in a blur. *Is this what our hospitals looked like 60 years ago?* Overcrowded patient rooms spilled over into the hallways, and spare mattresses lay strewn on the floor.

At the end of the tour, the doctor stopped by a large wooden door. He waited for the group to quiet down and began speaking in a quiet voice.

"Not all hospitals in Caracas are this poor. Some are as modern as you have in the States. Smaller villages have hospitals such as this. We do our best but unfortunately, we do not have room for the many, many people who need care. We are already above capacity and unable to help the people who need it."

Hannah remembered complaining once about the emergency room in Copper Ridge being slow. She wouldn't complain anymore.

Dr. Servisa continued, "The mud slides that devastated Caracas a few years ago swept through a small house behind the hospital and caused much damage to the hospital itself." He paused and took a deep breath as if to regain his composure. "We need to clean out the house so we may use it again. We would like to turn it into a small clinic." He threw a glance out the window behind him where a long line of needy people wrapped around the side of the building. "I need to get back to work. My wife, Francesca, will show you what to do."

He reached out his hand toward a petite woman walking quickly along the corridor. Her long hair was wrapped in a tight bun. "Francesca is a nurse here. She is the best there is."

Francesca spoke in halting English. "Your friend Hank will meet you in short time. He ask you start without him. I show you where."

The doctor faced the group. "Thank you—all of you—for coming. You are truly a blessing sent from God."

Hannah couldn't help herself. "Thank you for all you're doing, Dr. Cerveza."

The doctor and Francesca stopped and stared at her, looked at each other, and then broke into laughter. Hannah turned to Joelle, who only shrugged. The doctor was laughing so hard tears rolled down his face. "Servisa, dear. Not Cerveza. I'm not Doctor Beer."

● ● ●

"Well, I'll never complain about taking out the garbage again," Corey announced, dumping the rubble from his wheelbarrow onto the growing pile of debris.

"No kidding," agreed Gregg. "I mean, our basement is pretty messy—but it looks like Martha Stewart's house compared to this place." He waved at the devastated house, which was buried halfway up the walls with half-dug dirt piles.

"Martha Stewart?" teased Morgan. "Why, Gregg, I didn't know you were interested in girl stuff!"

"My mom watches it." Gregg's face turned red, and he shrank under Morgan's attention. "I watch . . . more manly things."

"I like the episode where Martha meets Arnold Schwarzenegger," Corey said.

"Oh, yeah," Lia said. "Didn't they bake a bomb and blow up all the cheap, out-of-style sofas?"

"Yes. The most beautiful bomb you've ever seen," Joelle sighed. "Covered in tailored blue gingham with a matching silk ribbon."

"C'mon, let's keep working," Hannah said. *What would the hospital staff think if they saw us standing around?*

"Oh, look at this." Valerie's face fell as she held up a little girl's shoe caked in hardened mud.

Everyone stopped, staring at the little symbol of life. Then they turned and continued to work soberly. Soon they uncovered a coffee table with a cup and saucer on it. Shredded clothes, a stroller. The stuff of life—monuments to the lives destroyed.

"What should we do with this stuff?" April asked. "Has anyone seen Hank yet?"

"Yeah, he's coming," Mercedes said, returning from the hospital restroom. "He's talking to Jared, who looks upset about something—no big surprise."

A metal door from the hospital swung open and clanged against the cinder-block wall. Jared burst through the door and charged up a hill. Hank came next, watching his son disappear over the other side of the hill. He turned and faced the quiet but curious group. He proceeded as though nothing were out of the ordinary.

"So far so good," he said, surveying the group's progress. He sighed.

Hannah thought it odd that he seemed to be gathering his composure. *What is that all about?*

Hank continued, "This house belonged to one of the nurses who worked at the hospital." His voice grew quieter. "She wanted to live close by in case they ever needed her help right away."

Hannah wanted to ask if the nurse had escaped the mud slide. But one look at Hank's face revealed the awful truth.

"It's possible you may come across some bones." Gasps rose from around the small room, and Mercedes dropped her shovel. "Although it's not probable. But if you do, just . . . stop digging and let me know." He regained his lighthearted composure. "Let's make a good start on this so the other teams can finish by the end of the week."

The group nodded, but no one sprang to action. Hannah's feet felt like stone. She'd already been through the emotional blender at the hospital. Now she had to dig in a house where people were buried alive?

Suddenly, Melanie appeared out of nowhere, touching her on the shoulder. "Do you want to help with sandwiches?"

Hannah jumped. "Yeah! Thanks," she said. She joined the sandwich assembly line inside the bus. Lia and Mercedes laughed and talked as they slathered rolls with peanut butter and jelly. Hannah took over slicing rolls open and half-listened to their conversation as she handed them off.

"Do you want to deliver these, Hannah?" Lia asked, handing her a stack of sandwiches. "The second round will be ready when you get back."

As Hannah, balancing a dozen sticky rolls on her tray, neared the house, a lump rose in her throat. A mud-caked doll lay crumpled against a pile of broken concrete. Hannah's feet slowed. An old broken picture frame sat nearby. The picture was distorted and smeared. A broken clock. A barrette. Shards of a blue plate. Hannah tried to swallow against the lump.

"Hannah, are you okay?" Joelle asked, looking at her intently.

Tears dripped down Hannah's face. She couldn't feel or speak.

"Here." Joelle took the sandwiches. "I'll take care of these. Go sit down for a while."

Hannah stumbled over to a nearby boulder. The other teens shoveled and pushed squeaking wheelbarrows around her.

"Can I get you anything?" Corey asked, stopping his loaded wheelbarrow in front of her.

Hannah didn't know how to answer. She felt pathetic. "I just need—"

Corey nodded. "It's pretty sad."

"I can't help it," she whimpered, wiping her eyes. "Here, let me help you."

"That's okay. It's pretty heavy."

Hannah noticed something peeking out of the rubble. It looked like a book.

"What's this?" She pulled it from the heap, brushing off the rubble.

"I don't know. I didn't see it when we loaded the barrow."

Dried mud covered the book on all sides. It cracked as she opened it. The words inside were mostly illegible. Dark water stains covered the few pages that would still separate.

"Not much to see," Hannah said, disappointed.

"Nope. I think it was a journal, though. If you look closely, you can see handwriting." He pointed to the page.

"Wow."

Hannah thought of her own journal—all the thoughts, prayers, and secrets. Someone had poured her heart into this raggedy book. The nurse perhaps? And now it would be discarded in a pile of dirt, stones, and broken dishes.

"Just goes to show how passing life is," she said. She stared at the cover of the book. The floral print on the cover—although faded—looked similar to the front of her own journal.

Joelle approached her. "The sandwiches are all handed out."

Hannah broke her contemplation. "Thanks, Joelle. I'll go get the next round."

She tucked the journal into her backpack and headed back to the bus.

chapter

Jacie struggled to sit up. It felt as though someone had dropped an anvil on her chest. She tried to swallow, but the effort and pain brought tears to her eyes. A gurgling knot moved around in her stomach. Perspiration dampened her hair, yet she curled into a ball to ward off the chills.

Sporadically, throughout the day, Jacie had tried to read, write in her journal, and draw. But with each attempt, she could sit up for only a few minutes at a time. Mostly, she weathered long, exhausting coughing fits and drifted in and out of sleep. The nurse visited every once in a while, dropped off colored pills, and reminded her to drink more water.

But now she felt waterlogged and in that awkward place between feeling weak and yet tired of sleeping. She swung her legs off the side of the couch to make another bathroom trip. But as soon as her feet hit the ground, her stomach started circling again and her head became lead. She fell back on her pillow. Staring up at the ceiling, Jacie released the pent-up tears.

Why is this happening? I'm no good here. I'm only dead weight. People didn't send me their hard-earned money so I could spend my days sick in a hotel room. She'd written in her support letter about all these wonderful things that she expected to happen, and now . . . well, now what would she say? "Thanks for sending in your gifts. You'll be happy to know, I am now an expert on Venezuelan hotel decor and have completed 300 charcoal drawings of the ceiling."

Dead weight. The thought rang in her head. She'd been an inconvenience from the moment she burst into this world. She was a burden to her mom, who could have been a famous journalist if she hadn't been stuck with Jacie.

And her dad? He handled the "burden" by inviting her into his life when it was convenient for him. It wasn't that he didn't love her. He did. And he was proud of her. The last time she went to visit him, he was so proud of her talent, he toted her along to cocktail parties to show her off.

But it wasn't enough to have him be proud of her. She wanted more from him—and she hated herself for it.

● ● ●

Jacie heard the laughter even before the door plowed open.

"I was not flirting with him," Lia shrieked. "I was only being friendly."

"Oh, puh-leeze," Natalie said. "How can you say that?"

"You might as well have plunked yourself down on his lap, girl-friend," Nichole said.

"I should've thought of that," Lia mused.

"I think doing your little dance was plenty," Hannah said.

"At least Hannah knows how to turn people down," Joelle said.

Lia turned to Jacie. "Hannah asked our interpreter how to say courtship in Spanish—"

"And he didn't understand, so Hannah kept telling all these guys that were hitting on her what the interpreter told her to say—" April stepped in.

"That she was taking them to court!" finished Celia.

"Well, it still worked. They left me alone," Hannah said, smiling.

"I need to go to the bathroom."

"Number one or number two? If number two, I'm going first."

"Y'mean we can't flush yet?"

"They said the water wouldn't be turned on until after dinner tonight."

Everyone groaned.

"Just hurry up. I've *got* to go."

"Laurilee, do you have any of those Pringles left? I'm starving."

"Can you believe I had four PB&J sandwiches today?"

Jacie slumped on the couch, half-listening to the girls' lively banter. She felt like a complete outsider. All the girls worked together that day, serving and bonding and making memories she would never be a part of. *Don't start in on a pity party, Jacie,* she chided herself.

The front door opened and Becca stuck her head inside. "Anyone going swimming?"

"I am!"

"Me, too!"

Lia emerged in a bathing suit with a towel slung over her shoulder. "Are you going swimming with us, Jacie?"

As much as she wanted to go, she could barely sit up. "I'd better not," she croaked, the words setting her sore throat on fire. She swallowed, willing the tickle in her chest to quit before it triggered another coughing fit.

"Jacie?" Becca said. She came across the room and plopped onto the floor next to her. "What's wrong?"

"I'm sick," she croaked.

"Why didn't anyone tell me?" Becca looked in Hannah's direction.

"I didn't know where to find you," Hannah said. "I told Tyler. He said he'd come check on her later after he put the sound system away." She sat next to Jacie. "Do you feel better at all?"

Jacie shrugged. "No. I feel worse." Tears blurred her vision. "My chest feels heavy and I'm coughing up—"

"Gross!" Kylie tapped her foot impatiently.

Becca stroked her hair. "Do you want me to stay with you?" she asked.

"I could stay too," Hannah offered.

Yes, please stay. I'm so lonely.

"No, that would be silly. You guys have had a long day. I'm just going to nap some more."

"Are you sure, darlin'?" Laurilee asked.

"Of course."

"Okay," Becca said hesitantly as the girls filed out. "I'll bring you dinner later."

"We'll be back really soon," Hannah called before she closed the door behind her.

Jacie listened to the giggling fade down the stairs. She fell back into a fitful sleep, barely noticing when Becca and Tyler brought her dinner. Both kissed her on her head before tiptoeing out. Sometime later she woke up to find herself alone . . . again.

● ● ●

Jacie's eyes popped open. She heard footsteps on the stairs. *Maybe the girls are coming back*, she thought. She propped herself up on the couch, feeling like a rag doll, then sighed as she realized the steps came from only one person.

A soft knock sounded at the door.

"Coming," she croaked. She wrapped herself in the blanket and shuffled to the door, hunched over like an old woman. She opened the door. "Berk?"

"Hi, Jacie. Can you come out in the hall for a minute? I want to talk to you."

"Sure." Was he going to suggest she go home since the only thing she was doing here was spreading germs? She pulled her blanket around her and plopped down on the orange-carpeted step, leaning against the wall for support. Berk sat next to her.

"Here. I brought you this." He held out a dripping Popsicle with a damp napkin wrapped around the stick. "I bought the biggest one the corner store had, knowing half of it would melt before I could get it to you."

Jacie took it from him. "Wow. Thanks." She unwrapped it, letting the icy coolness soothe her burning throat. Tears came to her eyes.

"Do you want me to go?" Berk asked, looking at her with concern.

She shook her head. "It's just that . . ." She sighed. "This was just really, really nice of you."

"You're welcome."

"Did you go to FUAGNEM?" Jacie asked, closing her eyes at each draw on the Popsicle. Pain and pleasure mixed together.

"Yes."

"Was it good?"

Berk smiled. "Susie talked."

Jacie smiled back. "Guess that means it was good." She drew her brows together. "So where is everybody?"

"Susie swapped things a little. She put worship before and after her talk. I ducked out the moment she finished. I kept thinking of you and how lonely you must be."

Jacie wanted to cry. *This* was how a dad was supposed to be. She headed off the tears with a question. "So tell me about it. What did she talk about tonight?"

"You're awfully sick. Are you sure you want to talk about God stuff?

Or do you just need to finish the Popsicle and go to bed?"

"I want to hear."

"Susie talked about taking a step beyond being saved."

Jacie cocked her head. "What do you mean?"

"Well. Most of us think that everything is done when we are saved. But that's just the beginning. One of the steps we need to take later is to be willing to be fully committed to serving God with our lives. One hundred percent. No matter what He asks of us."

"Wow."

"Yeah. It's a big step. Susie put it in the context of being a bond servant."

"I've heard that, but I don't really know what it means." Her heavy head ached. She longed to rest it on Berk's shoulder and have him tell her it would be all right.

"A bond servant is a slave who has been set free and yet chooses to remain a slave to the master in order to serve him for the rest of his life. He prefers serving the master to his own freedom."

"And that's what we're supposed to be," Jacie said quietly, examining the concept in her mind. She would love to live a life like that. But she doubted she ever could.

Berk opened his Bible. "She read some verses. This is the only one I remember: 'Having also believed you were sealed in Him with the Holy Spirit . . .'" He closed his Bible. "Susie explained it better than I can. Afterwards, she gave everyone a chance to pray and decide if they were willing to become a bond servant to Jesus Christ. If so, they could come up front."

Jacie nodded. She was glad she hadn't been there. She doubted her ability to make such a commitment.

"The kids who went up front were given these." He held up a black corded necklace. A small metal rectangle with symbols etched into it hung from the cord.

"What does it say?"

"It's Hebrew for 'Bond Servant of the Messiah.' In Biblical times, bond servants were pierced to show who they belonged to. This is a little easier way to kind of show the same thing. That we're bond servants to Christ."

Jacie stared at the necklace. *I know God wants and deserves all of me. But I don't think I can give that to Him. I'm too selfish. I'm too messed up. I'm too afraid. And I don't want to promise something and then take it back later.*

He paused. "It's for you if you want it. I wasn't going to give it to you until you got better. But since we're talking about it—"

The Popsicle dripped onto her hand. She licked it off. She looked at the necklace. She wanted to say "yes." She wanted to for Berk. She hated disappointing him. But she had to be honest. She had to want it for God, not for Berk.

"I can't," she said. "I'm not there yet."

Berk searched her, his eyes telling her to go on.

She took a deep breath and tried to explain. "Every camp and youth retreat I go on, I decide *this time* I'm going to live for God. *This time* I'm going to go back home and be bold about my faith. *This time* I'll spend hours reading my Bible and be obedient to all of God's commands. But every 'this time' ends in failure. I can't make such a huge promise to God when I don't think I can do it."

"Sometimes making the promise helps you to be faithful to it."

Jacie shook her head. She knew she couldn't be totally sold out. If she were, she'd be a lot bolder with Solana. She'd inundate her father with her faith. She'd be stumbling over the backpacks to have the chance to minister to Venezuelans. But that wasn't Jacie. She wasn't a sold-out kind of girl.

She bit her lip and looked at the rapidly melting Popsicle.

"It's okay," Berk said, putting his arm around her shoulder and pulling her close. "When the time is right, you'll know."

"Will I?" she asked. *I hope I will. But it doesn't seem very likely.*

J O U R N A L

Another day, another smelly, bumpy bus ride. It's strange not having Jacie with us. I miss her. We had to borrow a clown from another team for our performances. I don't understand why Melanie hasn't asked me to give the invitation yet. I thought I made it clear I was interested and willing to do it. I bet the other kids are too nervous to volunteer. But maybe if they see me do it, they'll see how God gives them the words to say.

"Melanie," Hannah said, sliding into the empty spot next to the leader. The seat felt sticky on the back of her legs. "Have you assigned someone to give the invitation today?"

"Corey asked to do it for the first performance." Melanie ran her fingers through her thick, short hair. "But no one's lined up for the second."

"I'll do it—if that's okay."

"I think that would be wonderful."

Excitement trilled through her. "Thanks!"

She stumbled her way to the back of the moving bus, dropping to the seat in front of Joelle and Mercedes. "I'm giving the invitation this afternoon," she told them.

Laurilee turned around in her seat. "You'll be great at that, Hannah! You're so articulate an' all."

"Thanks!" Hannah grinned. "I mean, I hope the Lord uses me."

"I'm sure He will," Joelle said.

Hannah leaned back. "I'm glad we have an interpreter. Even my simple Spanish words are horrible."

"Morgan and I could teach you some easy words," Mercedes said. She and Morgan had both taken several years of Spanish and were doing well communicating with the locals.

"Like what? I can't learn the whole gospel message in 10 minutes," lamented Hannah.

"Just conversational basics. 'Hello, how are you?' 'Where's the bathroom?'—that kind of stuff," said Mercedes.

"I know 'hello,'" said Hannah. "*Hola*."

"Good," said Joelle, smiling. "But next time don't pronounce the 'h.' Say it 'oh-la' instead of 'hole-uh.'"

They spent the rest of the bus trip learning words and phrases.

"Okay, so '*Jesus*' means 'Jesus,'" she said, pronouncing it "hey-suess." "*Baño*' means 'bathroom,' '*qué*' means 'what?,' '*sí*' is 'yes,' and '*no*' is 'no,'" Hannah reviewed. "That's pretty easy."

"When in doubt, just nod and say '*sí*,'" said Mercedes. "They're probably telling you how much they enjoyed the performance or about their family or whatever. They talk fast, so even if you did understand more, it's hard to catch it all."

Hannah nodded. "*Sí.*"

"Listen to that. You're practically fluent," Joelle grinned.

● ● ●

Hannah struggled to stay with the music cues while praying for the building crowd. She prayed as she concentrated on the motions and music, *Lord, help them understand.* She ran on tiptoe to her place as last in line behind the other toys, waiting for the Evil Magician to give each of them a gift.

The toys reeled and spun—sent into chaos under the Evil Magician's spell. When Hannah threw her whole self into the chaos, her spin fell out of control. She couldn't stop before spinning into the Baseball Player. The Baseball Player, already off balance and unaware of the spinning Princess behind her, fell face forward into the China Doll, who tripped and collided with the substitute Clown. The Clown, led by her awkward costume, ran into the Prince, who knocked over the Nurse, who toppled over the Evil Magician. The gifts scattered everywhere, and the characters lay on the cement, uninjured, but not knowing how to continue the performance.

Roaring laughter pummeled the scattered toys as the crowd presumed the comical collapse was part of the show.

Hannah pushed aside the sick feeling in her stomach over what she'd caused. She jumped to her feet, offering the Baseball Player a hand. All the actors scurried through the scene, failing to catch up with the music. As the performance went into turbo speed, Hannah couldn't figure out what she was supposed to be doing. She did everything wrong—coming on too late or moving in the wrong direction. She even ran into Jesus while he was being crucified.

"Excuse me," she said, shoving her way to the other side of the stage. Jesus gave her a nod of forgiveness. *How Christ-like.*

As the last scene closed, the actors froze, then formed a line to take a short bow. Tears stung Hannah's eyes. She looked straight ahead, not wanting to see the angry reactions of her teammates. And the crowd! *All those lives. There's no way they could have understood this was the gospel message. It looked more like a bunch of crazy-costumed kids randomly re-arranging themselves on a stage.*

Corey stepped up to the microphone.

Strangely enough, while Corey spoke, the audience appeared attentive—in fact, some people were crying! Her teammates didn't look at all angry.

"If any of you would like to accept this gift of life from the Toy-maker's Son, you only need to ask Him." Corey paused while the interpreter translated. "Please come forward if you would like to pray with us."

Hannah's mouth gaped as a flood of people moved to the front of the stage. The team cheered to welcome them.

"Good performance, Team 10!" Melanie called. "Now let's hit the crowd and share the Good News." A couple of kids stayed with Corey to pray with those who came forward, while the rest of them went to initiate conversations with those still in the crowd.

The enthusiastic herd moving into the audience swept Hannah along with them. *Okay, God, here goes. Please show me who You want me to talk to.* She searched for an interpreter, knowing it would be easier to converse with one by her side. But Carlos—a young man in a blue base-ball cap—was busy. She walked toward a tree to survey the scene. Maybe God would point to someone with a beam of light.

"*Hola*," said a man lounging at the foot of the tree. A brown paper bag with a half-eaten lunch rested on his lap. Shadows from the tree danced across his graying hair, and a wide grin adorned his face.

He's initiating a conversation. Hannah smiled at him. "*Hola*," she said, remembering what Joelle had said about the silent "h."

Hannah referred to her laminated yellow translation card. She slowly pronounced the first question on it, which asked the question "What did you think of the drama?"

The man was doing exactly as Mercedes had said—talking a mile a minute. Hannah nodded, smiled, and kept saying, "*Sí, sí.*" *This is easy. I can handle this.* She was building a relationship, and when an interpreter became available, they would be able to have a conversation about Christ.

She soon noticed the young man in the blue baseball cap edging around the crowd.

"Excuse me." Hannah held up a finger to indicate to her new friend she'd be back in a minute. She wove her way through the crowd, tapped the interpreter on his arm, and motioned for him to come over to her new friend.

"Ask him what he thought of the performance, please," she said when they returned to the tree.

The interpreter gave her a blank look.

Hannah repeated her question. *What is it? No one understands my English either?*

Mercedes sidled up next to Hannah, recognizing her uneasiness. "*Cómo se llama?*" she asked.

"Luis," the gray-haired man answered.

"Gualberto," said the other.

"Isn't he an interpreter?" asked Hannah, pointing to Gualberto.

Mercedes shook her head. "No, our interpreters are over there." She pointed toward a crowd near the stage. Sure enough, she saw Carlos talking excitedly with a group of children, his cap bouncing up and down with enthusiasm.

"Sorry," she said to Gualberto, her face growing red.

"*Lo siento,*" said Mercedes, then asked another question in her slow Spanish.

Luis replied, pointing excitedly at Hannah.

"What did he say?" asked Hannah.

Mercedes sucked in her cheeks, obviously struggling to keep a straight face. "Apparently, you agreed to marry him."

"What? No, tell him I can't. Tell him I . . . I just can't."

Mercedes said something else to Luis. He shook his head and asked a question.

Hannah gripped Mercedes's arm. "Does he understand?"

"He's persistent," Mercedes smirked. "He wants to know what will convince you to marry him—what you want as a promise."

This isn't supposed to happen. I'm supposed to be sharing God's love with people—not hurting their feelings or rejecting them. I have to make him understand—without being mean.

She turned to Luis, his eyes eager to hear her answer. She wanted to explain about courtship and Christianity and why she couldn't marry him because she lived in a different country and was only 17. She wanted to clarify there was nothing he could offer her that would make her change her mind. But she hardly knew what to say in English— much less in Spanish. With her hands flailing in non-descript body language, her newly-learned words of *qué*, *sí*, and *no* became mixed into one word. "*Queso! Queso!*"

Gualberto looked confused. Mercedes looked confused. Luis looked down at his sandwich, lifted up the top, and peeled off a piece of cheese. He shrugged and held it up to Hannah.

"*Queso* means 'cheese,' Hannah," murmured Mercedes.

Oh, brother.

● ● ●

The story came out as the group set up a picnic in the park for lunch. Everyone enjoyed Mercedes's animated version of Hannah trying to convince Luis that she couldn't marry him—and no amount of cheese would convince her.

"Some girls want guys who are handsome and rich. Hannah just wants someone with cheese," Lia added as Mercedes wrapped up the story.

Corey knelt on one knee next to Hannah's picnic bench. "Darling, I don't have money for a diamond ring, but I can offer you either Swiss or cheddar."

"C'mon, Corey," joined in Morgan. "Hannah's a girl of high standards. The least you can do is propose to her with Brie."

"I can see the singles ad now," Laurilee said in a dreamy voice. "Single young woman in search of single man. Enjoys long walks on the beach, candlelight dinners, and sharing dairy products."

"Lactose intolerant need not apply," added Valerie.

Hannah dove into the fun. "What's wrong with that? Strong bones and healthy teeth are attractive," she grinned.

"Well, now that you're betrothed, Hannah, we'll have to start planning the wedding. Where are you registered?" asked April.

"Probably Kraft," piped up Phoebe.

The teasing continued, but Hannah silently prayed, *Please, God, help someone lead that poor man to You. Forgive me for messing up. Help me do better at the next performance. Give me strength and courage to boldly proclaim Your truth. And please give me a great response.*

● ● ●

In an impoverished *barrio*, about 60 people crowded around the small raised platform being used as a makeshift stage to watch the opening skits. As Hannah prayed for the second performance, she looked in awe around her. The stench of decay and filth permeated the air. Most wore clothing Goodwill wouldn't even sell.

In spite of the noise from the busy intersection behind them, the audience watched, craning their necks to see what was happening. *Ready to be harvested*, Hannah thought to herself.

When the skits were finished, Berk introduced the performance, Melanie hit the play button, and the show began.

As Hannah went through her Princess motions, she could see that the crowd appeared enthralled. Excitement coursed through her. Finally, as the last notes of the song dwindled, the crowd cheered and applauded. The team lined up to take their final bow while Hannah prayed like mad. The performance was so good, she knew the response would be even better. She strode up to center stage, and the interpreter handed her a microphone.

"Thank you for watching," she began, and the interpreter repeated the words in Spanish.

Hannah spoke with confidence. She explained in great detail who each of the performers in the drama represented. She hadn't meant for it to be so long, but she kept thinking of more things to share.

"It tells us in the Gospel of John, verse 16 of chapter three, that God loved us so much He sent His son to die for us." Hannah paused, waited for the interpreter, and then continued. "Now you may be wondering why He had to do that. It's because we were all on our way to hell because of the sin in our lives."

She started into her definition of hell, but she noticed Berk's eyebrows shoot up and decided against going into a full explanation.

"Hell is a bad place with a lake of fire."

Some folks started to get restless. People on the fringes of the crowd began to move away. Melanie motioned for her to wrap it up.

"Wait!" she called to the stragglers. "You can't leave yet. This is the most important decision of your life." But they ignored her, continuing to move toward something more interesting.

She quickly wrapped up the message. "Would anyone like to come forward and ask Christ into your life? I would be very happy to pray with you."

She waited impatiently for the interpreter. But even after he finished, the crowd remained still. A few people got up and Hannah smiled, but they only turned to leave.

What was wrong? Why weren't people responding? Had the interpreter said the right thing?

"That means you can come up now," she repeated with increased urgency. "You can accept Christ today. I'd love to pray with you."

Melanie instructed the group to mingle in the crowd and do one-on-one evangelism with their cards. Hannah found herself in the middle of the scrambling throng, stunned.

Joelle sidled up next to her. "Remember, Hannah, the seeds were planted. Even if there isn't an immediate response, God is still working."

Hannah nodded. But if God was working, He certainly wasn't doing it through her.

chapter 14

Roses are red,
Vilets are Blue,
Puking is gross
And spreds germs too.
Get off your lazy bum and get back to work.
From, the Gregg-mann

Jacie refolded the construction paper. At first she thought it was sweet that Gregg had dropped off the homemade card before the team left that morning. But that was before she opened it. *I'm about ready to slug "The Gregg-mann,"* thought Jacie.

Jacie settled on the couch and drank the last gulp of water in her glass. It felt like fire going down her throat. *But I need to drink lots of water to get better,* she reminded herself. And she desperately wanted to feel better. She wanted to be with everyone else—ministering and making memories together.

God, did You want me to come on this trip? I thought Your voice was so clear. But maybe I imagined it. What do I know about Your voice anyway? Is my being sick Your way of telling me I'm not supposed to be here? You could've told me sooner, God. Or was I just not listening?

She threw her pen across the room and sighed. She dreaded another day sitting in the muggy apartment all by herself. *There's not even a TV to watch*, Jacie thought glumly. At least that would trick her mind into believing there were people around. She stumbled into the kitchen and opened the refrigerator. The jug of purified water stood empty. *Of course*, she thought. *What else could go wrong?* There was plenty of water to be had—18 floors down in the dining area.

Jacie ambled down the stairs, clutching the rail with one hand and her water bottle in the other. The dizzy spells came less frequently, but she still feared tumbling down the stairs. Every couple of flights, she'd sit for a few minutes and lean her heavy head against the railing. Once on the ground floor, she stumbled through the lobby, then stepped out into a courtyard filled with sunshine and chirping birds. It seemed wrong that the rest of the world could be so happy when she felt so miserable.

Shuffling her way into the large dining room, she looked around for one of the big water containers. Nothing . . . no one . . . except . . .

"Jared?"

The figure hunched over a table straightened and turned around. "Jacie, what are you doing here?"

She held up her empty water bottle. "Looking for water. What about you?"

"Can't a guy sit and think?"

Harshness edged his voice, and Jacie almost turned around and left. *I don't have the energy to deal with this.* But something inside her wouldn't allow her to walk out.

"I thought you were working out at the site today," she said, pulling out a chair across from him and sliding into it.

"I told Dad yesterday I'm not going to help out with the teams any-more."

Jacie focused on a moth that kept banging itself against a window pane, relentlessly trying to get inside. "Don't they need you? It seems like we have so few interpreters as it is—"

"Why do you care?" He stood up and the folding chair dropped with a clatter onto the tiled floor. "Are you going to be my mother and tell me what to do?"

"No," Jacie sighed. She dropped her head onto the table, her fore-head hitting it with a soft thud. She lay her fevered cheek against the cool surface, waiting for the room to stop spinning. "Jared," she said, "I don't understand."

"I'm not asking you to."

Jacie held up her hand to quiet him. "I don't understand why you've been so rude to everyone. I don't think any of us have done anything to deserve it." She paused. Dare she ask? "What is it, Jared? What's mak-ing you so angry?"

"You don't have to play the Christian role, Jacie. You don't need to pretend you care."

Jacie shook her head, feeling a surge of indignation. "I know I have flaws, but pretending to care about people when I really don't isn't one of them." Her tone sharpened. "You have every right to sit here and sulk if that's what you want to do. But you don't have the right to make judgments about me. You don't even know me."

Jared seemed as surprised by the outburst as Jacie was. "And you don't know me either." He gritted his teeth. "You don't know what my life is like."

"You're right. But does that mean I can't care?"

Silence.

"Why don't you tell me then?"

He practically spat the words. "Because it won't fit into your happy little Christian mind-set."

Jacie almost laughed. "What makes you think I have a happy little Christian mind-set? I can tell you right now I am anything but happy. My ideal life is constantly being yanked away from me. To add to my long list of disappointments, I come on a mission trip to serve God and instead I'm sick, stuck up in my room feeling sorry for myself the last two days. So if you like, we can just sit here and be miserable together." She dropped her head to the table again. She focused on the stupid moth. *Thunk. Thunk.*

Jared cleared his throat. "Have you ever wanted to be with someone you love, but it's impossible?"

"Yeah. My dad. Every single day."

Jared stared at her. He cleared his throat. "Okay. The woman I loved . . ." He paused.

"What?" Jacie's heart melted in an instant. She lifted her head.

He turned away. The moth beat against the window, relentless.

"Jared, I'm so sorry." She hesitated, remembering the name he'd called her the first day. "Marisa?"

Jared smiled sadly. "Yeah. She looked like you a bit—same springy curls and chocolate-milk complexion. That's what she called it, *'leche de chocolate.'* "

He took a breath. Swallowed. Jacie waited for him to continue.

"She was amazing. She had this contagious laugh, and the most generous heart." He paused. "And a precious daughter."

He smiled at something far away. "Angela, her little girl, called me *'oso,'* which means 'bear' in Spanish. I would crawl after her, growling. She'd laugh so hard."

"That's so sweet," Jacie said. The picture of Jared playing with a little girl made her smile.

"Marisa started calling me *'oso'* too. But she said it was because of my big bear hugs." Jared shook his head to bring himself to the present. "I grew up in a Christian home, but until I met Marisa it was just something that I did. It wasn't real. Her deep love for God showed in everything she did. You couldn't be around her and not feel God's presence in spite of the fact that she'd been to hell and back."

"Hell and back?"

"Her father—a U.S. military pilot—abandoned the family when she was only a baby. Her mom died shortly after, so her aunts raised her. Marisa married young. Everyone hoped Marisa would have a better life with this American. But when their little girl was six months old, the jerk bolted just like Marisa's father had."

"Wow." Jacie felt an immediate connection. *Two fatherless girls . . .*

Jared looked at her. "I don't think anyone has ever just sat and let me talk about Marisa without giving me some 'good Christian response.' "

"I don't have any of those. She had a hard, hard life. There's nothing I can say to make it any less awful."

Jared sat with a faraway look in his eyes. Jacie waited.

"Marisa's two aunts became very protective. Soon, her Aunt Carlita forbade her from seeing me," he said.

"Why?"

"I was American. Marisa's father and husband were Americans too."

"But you saw her anyway?"

"We met in secret." He smiled at the memory. "We had a few close calls at the marketplace downtown. I had to hide behind the mangoes more than once. One day, Aunt Carlita caught us at a café. She was furious! She took hold of Marisa's arm and Angela by the hand and dragged them both out."

"Oh, no."

"Marisa came to me early that evening. Her aunts had given her an ultimatum: Either give me up or be disowned."

Jacie's mouth dropped.

"Family is everything here," Jared continued. "Especially for Marisa. They'd taken care of her since she was a baby. They were all she and Angela had."

Jared shook his head. His voice broke as he spoke. "She was willing to give them up for me. But I couldn't let her do it. Angela played on the floor while we argued, and I kept watching her. I couldn't make up for the love she would lose without the family. I couldn't do it."

Jacie felt a stabbing pain.

"We fought. I told her it was over. I said things I didn't mean just to drive her away. I sent her home, telling her I never wanted to see her again. That's the hardest thing I've ever had to do."

"Do you think it was a mistake?"

"Absolutely."

Jacie grabbed Jared's arm. "Why don't you go back to her? Tell her how you feel?"

"I can't, Jacie," he said grimly.

"Jared, don't be ridiculous. Let go of your pride or . . . whatever it is. Of course you can go back. You can always go back."

"No!" Anger stirred his eyes. "She's dead, Jacie." His voice was ice. "I sent her home and a mud slide destroyed everything that same night." He dropped his head into his hands. "There is no way to go back."

A lump rose in Jacie's throat. She could only be silent while Jared stared out the window and wiped away the occasional tear.

Tears poured down her own cheeks. "Jared," she whispered, "I don't know what to say. I'm so sorry."

He stared at her. Studied her.

Jacie let the tears slide down her face and drop onto the table. "Did her daughter die too?" she asked, afraid for the answer.

He nodded.

"Oh, Jared . . ."

"I've wished a million times I could redo that evening. Tell her I'm sorry. That I love her. I didn't mean any of it."

Jacie felt as though a piece of her own heart had been torn away.

He turned to look out the window. "I need to go pack. We're leaving the hotel after Dad gets back today."

He strode off. Jacie racked her brain for something to say—words of comfort or understanding. She wanted to call after him, but what could she tell him? She had no concept of that kind of pain. He'd poured out his heart to her and she'd given him nothing in return.

Will I ever say something right? Will I ever help people instead of hurting them? She thought of Damien, the painting, and the art show. *Why do I always screw things up?*

She stood up and stared outside. The moth lay still on the window sill.

● ● ●

Jacie was still staring out the same window an hour later when the team arrived.

Gregg entered the dining hall, carrying an empty water jug in each hand.

"Oh, I get it, Jell-O Cube," he said. "You're feeling great. You just want to sit around all day and pretend you're sick."

Jacie shook her head. She didn't have the energy to argue. In truth, she felt worse than ever.

"Actually, you must not be faking because everyone got sick today. Morgan, Mercedes, and April were all dizzy. And a bunch of others are getting sore throats. We had to call off our second performance." He coughed. "I guess you infected us all."

Jacie's jaw dropped. *No. I didn't.* "I'm so sorry . . ." she whispered.

Gregg burst out in laughter. "I can't believe you actually fell for that! You are sooo gullible!" He held his sides and laughed.

Jacie could feel the heat in her face, the hardness in her stomach. She couldn't contain it. The boiling pot of emotion inside erupted. "Gregg, you . . . you . . . that's not funny. Why do you have to be so annoying? I don't want to look at you!"

Gregg's mocking grin collapsed. He turned and left without a word.

"I can't believe you said that, Jacie."

Jacie turned toward the voice. Corey stood in the open doorway, two empty water bottles hung at his sides. His eyes narrowed.

"I just can't deal with him. I just—he's annoying me on purpose."

"Trust me, I share a room with the guy. I know he can be a little obnoxious. But anyone can see he's got a thing for you. And you treat him subhuman?"

Jacie sat in stunned silence.

Corey continued, "I thought you were bigger than that."

See what happens when you get out of bed?

Corey set his water bottles on the table and walked out.

And Jacie tried not to envy the moth.

chapter

Team 10 clustered around the front of the stage. But not Hannah. She sat as far away as she could, an invisible wall separating her from the rest of the teams. *They* laughed and joked, happy with how the day had gone. *They'd* led people to the Lord. God was using *them*.

Scenes from earlier in the day continued to play in her mind. Smirking faces. Laughter. No one had responded. *No one. Why did I bother to come?*

As worship began, she stayed disconnected—as if God had descended onto everyone else and missed her. Groups of girls had their arms around each other, swaying to the music. Others had their hands stretched up in passionate worship. Hannah felt like an uninvited party guest.

God, You say we're not supposed to be at home in this world. And whenever I feel awkward or misplaced, I remember that. But here where I should be comfortable, connected, and alive, I'm an outsider. God, don't You care about me?

The songs of adoration grated on her raw soul. She slid out the back doors and climbed the narrow steps to the pool area. Muted voices filtered up from below. She leaned against the chain-link fence that surrounded the iridescent green swimming pool, a bright moon reflecting on its surface. She gazed at the sparkling city of Caracas and let her pent-up emotions escape. Hesitant tears gave way to full-blown sobs.

I was supposed to be a leader on Team 10. I was supposed to pray with lots of people and introduce them to Christ. I was supposed to be the one the other girls confided in and learned from. I was supposed to be the good Christian role model.

God, all I want to do is serve You and do Your will. Don't You want to use me?

She recalled a conversation she'd had with Jacie about prayer the first day they were in Miami. *Is that how God really is?* Jacie asked. *He won't give us things until we ask enough times? Maybe 999 times won't be enough, but once we ask the thousandth time He'll give in?*

She sank into a white plastic pool chair and buried her face in her hands. She knew she'd probably prayed more than anyone on her team about the trip—so why were they getting all the results? *Did I just not ask enough times, God?* Streams of tears trailed down her arms and spotted the cement patio.

Surprise words came suddenly to mind, and she looked around to see if someone had spoken them.

Why do you think your plans are what I want you to do?

Was this God's voice? Or was her mind playing tricks on her? If God hadn't shown that He cared so far, why would He show up now?

Why do you think your plans are My will?

"Because it says in Your Word that You want us to go out into all the world and preach the gospel to every creature," she said softly. "And that's what I'm trying to do—" She thought of her goal list. "—and more."

That's what you're trying to do?

"Right. I'm obeying Your commands. So that means You should be rewarding my obedience with results."

Really?

"Yes. Because You care about the lost. You don't want anyone to be lost for eternity."

That's right.

"And here I am, eager to be used by You to be an example and to bring others into Your kingdom."

And you're sure this is My plan for you.

"Of course."

My ways are above your ways, My thoughts above yours.

"Yeah, but something is broken." She said the words aloud now.

Was God laughing?

Maybe according to you. But according to Me, everything is as it should be.

"That doesn't make sense," she muttered.

"What doesn't make sense, Hannah?" came a deep voice in the dark.

Hannah's mouth dropped. "God?"

An embarrassed voice behind her said, "Uh, no. It's me, Berk."

"Berk?" Hannah instantly became aware of how pathetic she must look—talking to herself, sporting a tear-stained face. Her clumsy explanation tumbled out. "I'm sorry. I needed to get a breath of fresh air. I didn't mean to skip out." *Great. I am trying to prove to the leaders that I'm responsible and here one finds me ditching the evening meeting.*

"It's okay, Hannah." Berk sat in the chair next to her. "Is there anything you'd like to talk about? I'd love to listen."

Hannah stared out toward the city lights. She wanted to tell him everything. She wanted to ask him if she was bad. If she had unconfessed sin.

She couldn't do it. *He'll feel awkward and I'll feel faithless. And he'll probably think less of me if he finds out I'm the only one who hasn't led someone to the Lord.*

"No. Thanks, though. I just felt like I needed to pray for tomorrow. There are so many people in this city who need the Word," she gestured toward the skyline.

"Yes, there are," Berk agreed, but a look in his eye said he didn't really believe that's what she'd been pondering.

"I suppose I should probably head back downstairs again," she said before he could suggest it.

Berk didn't appear concerned. "Take your time, Hannah. But please know that both Melanie and I are here if you need anything." He tousled her hair and retreated into the dark.

I have to pull myself together, determined Hannah.

After splashing some pool water on her red, splotchy face, she made her way back to FUAGNEM.

Hannah slipped through the back door. Susie stood on stage, telling the story of Cain and Abel. Hannah knew the story backward and forward. The brothers had both offered sacrifices to God. Abel presented his best lamb, and Cain offered a selection of vegetables from his garden. But God had only been pleased with Abel's gift.

"Cain became angry," Susie was saying, clutching a bundle of carrots. She whined, imitating Cain. "God, You were supposed to like *my* sacrifice. It's good. Why isn't it good enough for *You?*"

Hannah recognized that question. She had asked it earlier that day when no one responded to her invitation.

Susie walked to the front of the stage and scanned the audience. "Think about it, guys . . . girls. How many times have we decided that we want things to happen in our own way? Or pushed things to happen in our own time?"

Hannah shifted as Susie continued.

"What if we say, 'Okay, God, I'll fast all day Sunday and Monday; volunteer at the homeless center Tuesday, Wednesday, and Thursday;

and do street evangelism every Friday and Saturday.' The church looks at that and goes, 'Wow, God must be really happy with that.'"

She paused and stared right at Hannah. "Aren't those *good* things?"

Hannah smiled. She tried to do all those things. A slide show played in her mind—serving at the Community Center, playing in the church orchestra, evangelizing the cashier at the grocery store.

Susie held the bunch of carrots over her head. "Cain thought his sacrifice was good. But it wasn't what God asked for. Cain's own choice of what to sacrifice showed his defiant heart against God. What did God really want? It says in the Word that obedience is better than sacrifice. What does that mean? It means that what we offer God is wrong if it's our own choice instead of His.

"'But, Susie,' you say, 'I give my time, money, talents to the church . . .' Great! But if you're living in pride over all you do for God and you don't bother to really have a relationship with Him," Susie paused, her voice going soft, "then all you do doesn't matter."

● ● ●

"The Ooga what?" Hannah peeked through the open bedroom door.

"The Ooga-Booga Club," repeated April impatiently, twisting a strand of curly red hair. "C'mon, you have to join. It's fun."

"I'm busy right now, but thanks—" Hannah began to close the door.

"Don't let her turn you down, April!" Joelle's laughing words came from the living area. "We'll come drag her out if we have to."

"Well, you better start pulling the troops together, 'cause she's going to put up a fight," April called back, sticking her foot in the door frame so Hannah couldn't shut it.

"Really, you guys go ahead without me. You can tell me about it later," Hannah said.

"We're all havin' a fine ol' time out here, won'tcha come join us?"

Hannah heard the lilting accent before Laurilee's heart-shaped face peered around the hallway entrance.

"C'mon, Hannah. What could be more important than bonding with your fellow Team Tenners?" Mercedes's long hair hung upside down as the lanky girl leaned over the armrest of the couch, the strands sweeping the floor.

"I'm journaling and stuff. Doing my devotional for tomorrow," she replied.

She turned her back on the door and flopped down on the bed. She almost envied Jacie for being sick—they'd moved her into the one-person cubby off the kitchen so she could sleep undisturbed. Hannah opened her journal and started doodling with her pen.

Suddenly the door burst open. The clamoring girls swarmed over her and covered her with sheets and blankets.

"What are you doing?" The fabric layers muffled Hannah's question.

"Kidnapping you, of course," came a fake deep voice that sounded a little too much like Joelle.

Hannah soon realized struggling wasn't going to do much good. It only increased her entanglement in the mass of sheets. She felt herself slide off the bed.

"You guys, stop it! What if I break my tailbone or something?" she complained and laughed at the same time.

The kidnappers dragged her into the living area—accidentally bumping into a few walls along the way.

"Hey, watch it. I think that was her head!" an unidentified voice said.

"Hannah, are you okay?" another voice asked.

Hannah nodded before she realized they couldn't see her. "Yeah."

"Okay," said Phoebe. "On the count of three, we'll lift her up on the couch. One . . . two . . . three."

Hannah felt herself being dropped onto the couch and the layers of coverings being removed. She was still laughing. "You girls are crazy!" she said.

"Of course. That's what happens when you join the Ooga-Booga Club. Are you ready?" Valerie said as she motioned toward a couple of chairs nearby.

"I guess," Hannah said.

"Okay, stand in front of that chair and mirror everything I do," Jill explained, standing in front of the second chair.

Hannah hesitantly agreed.

Jill ran in place, yelling, "Ooga-Booga!"

Hannah ran in place. "Ooga-Booga?"

Jill did three jumping jacks. "Ooga-Booga!"

Hannah did three jumping jacks. "Ooga-Booga."

Jill bent at the knees and touched the floor. "Ooga-Booga!"

Hannah mirrored her, growing less tentative. "Ooga-Booga!"

Jill leaned to the right. "Ooga-Booga!"

Hannah started to laugh. "Ooga-Booga!"

Jill plopped back into her chair. "OOGA-BOOGA!"

Hannah plopped down in hers. *Cold. Wet. Squishy.* A light flashed.

"Eeeeek!" she squealed and jumped up, spinning around to see what she'd sat on. A sopping wet rag lay on the seat.

The other girls burst out laughing.

"Did y'all see that?" Laurilee shouted, dancing in little circles.

"That expression was priceless," said Lia.

"I got it on film," Nichole said, holding up a camera.

"Don't worry, Hannah," Joelle said. "We all had to do it." Hannah remembered the squeals earlier that night. Now she understood.

She laughed, "My bum's all wet."

"Join the Ooga-Booga Club," said Nichole. She and a few other girls turned to show Hannah their wet spots.

April fell back on the couch. "This is so great, you guys! I wish I had good friends like you back home."

"Amen to that!" Laurilee said, collapsing next to her.

"You don't?" Lia asked, taking a pillow and flopping on the floor with it.

"Nope. I rededicated my life to Christ about six months ago and realized the friends I had weren't the kind of influence I wanted in my life."

"Do you have new friends now?" Hannah inquired.

"Sort of. I mean, I mostly hang out with my church friends. I kinda hate to admit this, but I miss my old friends. They knew me better and were nicer, y'know?"

Hannah didn't understand. "But your old friends weren't believers, right? How could they know you well if they don't understand your faith?"

"Well, I know, but," April paused. "It's hard to explain."

Joelle jumped in. "It sounds like they knew you well enough to see your faults and accept you anyway."

"Yeah, exactly," April agreed. "I guess I don't really feel accepted by the group at church. They're not rude or mean or anything. I just feel like I'm not good enough, so I have to play a part when I'm with them."

"Been there, done that," said Morgan.

Morgan feels that way? thought Hannah. *But she's perfect.*

"I always think everyone at school is laughing at me behind my back," said Jill. "I'm constantly worried that I'm not wearing the right thing or that I'm doing something stupid."

"I feel that way too," Nichole laughed. "It's like there's some underground conspiracy. People saying, 'Okay, be nice to Nichole, but did you see what she did to her hair? It's horrible!'"

"Ha! I thought I was the only one who thought that!" said Valerie.

"Really? But you're beautiful," said Nichole.

"Well so are you!" Valerie retorted.

"My friends support me," Laurilee said softly. "It's my family who beats me up." She looked up, struggling to keep her tears in check. "I mean, they don't hit me or anything. They hit me with their words." She began to sob. Mercedes shoved a box of tissues into her lap, and Hannah stroked her back. "I'm sorry," Laurilee choked out.

"It's okay to cry," Joelle assured her.

"My dad tells me I'm fat, or that I'm ruining the family. Mom says I'm not smart enough to go to college." She paused. "Everything I do is wrong."

"How can you think that?" Phoebe asked. "You're wonderful."

"Todd tells me that." Laurilee smiled a half smile. "He's my boyfriend. He always believes in me."

"I'm glad you have somebody," Jill said.

Laurilee sighed, dabbing at her nose with a soggy tissue. "He's been great but—" She shrugged, crumpling the tissue in her hand.

"Yes?" encouraged Mercedes.

"Whenever I feel down or get into a fight with my parents, I call or go see him. He holds me so tight and says things I need to hear."

The group waited silently for her to continue.

Laurilee took a deep breath and exhaled. "But . . . it felt so good to be loved that I started letting him become more physical. We've never had sex, but we have done . . . a lot of things we shouldn't."

Hannah bit her tongue to keep from making a case for courtship. She'd talk to Laurilee about it later. "Why don't you break up with him?"

"I know I should." Laurilee stared at her hands. "But I don't know what I would do without him. How can I let go of the only person who seems to think I'm worth something?"

Hannah sank her teeth so hard into her tongue, it almost bled.

Joelle spoke tenderly, "I know, Laurilee. But shouldn't we try to do what is most holy—what is most pleasing to God, no matter how hard it is?"

Hannah grimaced. *That was my line.*

"It's just so hard to go backwards." Laurilee sounded small and vulnerable. "It doesn't seem fair to tell him I've changed my mind."

"It's sin," Hannah piped up. "And we have to flee from sin."

April nodded. "But that's easier said than done."

"Without Todd," Laurilee asked, "who else would accept me?"

Hannah listened as the other girls shared their feelings of inadequacy and insecurity. She couldn't understand much of their hurt. She'd always felt loved, and she couldn't imagine how it would feel to be unloved.

"And then," Celia said, "you start doing stupid things to be accepted by people you don't even care about."

"Like losing weight as if you'll never be skinny enough," Joelle said.

"Yeah, exactly." Celia looked up at Joelle. "How'd you know?"

Joelle hugged her knees up to her chin and gave Celia a sad smile. "I was anorexic for almost two years."

"Really?" Celia and Hannah said in unison.

Joelle nodded. "Really." She turned to Hannah. "Does that surprise you?"

Hannah didn't know what to say. Of course it surprised her. Anorexia was something only insecure, weak girls struggled with, right? And Joelle was ... well ... *strong*. Besides, how could anyone stop eating?

"As a ballet dancer, I felt lots of pressure to be stick thin. Even though I wasn't overweight, I felt huge compared to the professional dancers I admired."

"But how could you ever think that? You're so thin," said Valerie.

"I was even thinner then. Thirty pounds thinner."

Several girls gasped. Hannah's mouth dropped open. Joelle had the perfect dancer's body—slender arms, legs, and a tight torso. Joelle would be too skinny if she weighed even five pounds less than she did now. But 30 pounds?

"I would get such a high from the huge accomplishment of not eating anything all day."

croutons for breakfast

"I go the other way," admitted Laurilee. "I eat whenever I feel like life isn't worth living. I either eat or mess around with Todd to feel better. I guess if my body feels good, I can escape the pain for a little while."

Hannah wanted to speak words that would be helpful. It was a perfect opportunity to achieve one of her goals by making an impact on her team. *What would Jesus say in this situation?*

"We have to remember," she jumped in, "that our bodies are the temples of the Holy Spirit, and we should treat them with respect. Not carelessly. That's disobedience, and like Susie said tonight, how can God bless disobedience?"

The girls stared at Hannah.

"Of course He can't," Laurilee said, monotone. "I should go to bed. I feel silly for talking so much."

"You're not silly," Joelle said. "And you didn't talk too much. We all do things we shouldn't when we're feeling insecure."

Laurilee busied herself getting a glass of water. "Not all of us—"

The other girls gradually excused themselves to get ready for bed. Hannah wrapped her arms around her knees and stared at her toes. She had only wanted to help—share God's truth. *What happened?*

She sat in the living room by herself, waiting for everyone to finish in the bathrooms. One by one, the girls snuggled under sheets, turned out lights, and said good night.

Then Hannah slipped into the bathroom. She brushed her teeth, staring at herself in the cracked mirror. She looked normal enough. Why was she so awkward and irritating? She spat in the sink and poured bottled water over her brush to rinse it.

In bed, Hannah felt restless. She wanted to toss and turn, but she forced herself to hold still so she wouldn't wake Joelle, who slept next to her. The conversations replayed in her mind. *It's not that big of a deal, right? Laurilee probably won't even remember it tomorrow.* But an inner nagging drove her from bed to find her notebook.

Dear Laurilee,

Thanks for being so honest with us. I'm sorry for my insensitive response. I was so surprised to hear that you have doubts about your worth, because to me—and so many others—it's so clear that you are precious, sweet, and fun. I know God made you for a purpose and thinks you're incredible. You're His daughter—and that's more significant than being the smartest or the most athletic or anything. I know this may just sound like a bunch of fluff to you, but I keep picturing God watching you sleep tonight and being sad about what your parents say and that you don't understand how much He loves you. He wouldn't have created you the way you are otherwise. My prayer for you is that, like Paul said, you'll understand "how deep, wide, and long is the love of Christ."

Love,
Hannah

Hannah folded the piece of paper into a square and silently made her way into the living room. She found Laurilee's Bible and slipped the note inside.

chapter 16

The Team 10 bus trundled along the city streets. Those in the back sang choruses. Jacie wanted to join in, but her still-raw throat wouldn't allow it. Instead, she settled for scribbling in her journal, the pen jumping up a line every time the bus hit a bump.

> I'm finally back with the team—still sick, but at least able to function. I'm sitting alone, and I hate it. Hannah is in deep conversation with Laurilee. Gregg and Corey won't talk to me. Everyone else has either forgotten who I am or they don't want to get sick. In just two days there are new inside jokes and shared memories that I know nothing about.
>
> I hope I remember how to be a clown—

Deep in her chest a feather fluttered in her lungs. It tickled. And wiggled. *Oh no.* She coughed to make it stop. The more she coughed, the more it fluttered. Her eyes dripped tears. Her nose ran. She gagged. She scrambled in her backpack for a sucker, hoping it would soothe and stop the tickle. And she coughed and coughed and coughed.

● ● ●

The nearly barren park baked beneath a merciless sun. Despite the heat, most of the crowd remained after the performance. Some people just watched, while others stood in small groups, talking with teammates. *Everyone's become an expert at sharing the gospel,* Jacie thought. *Except me.* She noticed many of her friends no longer needed their laminated yellow cards to ask their questions.

"Come with me," Hannah insisted, tugging on Jacie's arm.

Jacie remembered the last time she'd been paired with Hannah to evangelize at a youth training conference. It had been a horrible, humiliating experience. "I can't do it, Hannah."

"Of course you can. Lia will watch the bags," Hannah persisted.

Lia saluted. "You can count on me."

Jacie looked around at the crowd. They looked like piranhas, all of them, ready to devour her at a moment's notice. She clutched her cheater card and the words blurred together. "I think I'll faint."

"You won't faint," Hannah said, dragging Jacie toward the crowd.

"I'm still sick. I might cough on them," Jacie sputtered. "My throat really hurts. I don't think I should talk."

"Trust me." She moved Jacie around the edges of the horde. "We both learned something at the art show."

Jacie nodded as if she understood, but she wondered what in the world Hannah meant.

"Here we are," Hannah said, stopping in front of some little girls playing hopscotch. Morgan and Valerie hopped with them.

Morgan and Hannah exchanged smiles. Then Morgan took the

hand of a little girl and spoke in slow Spanish, pointing behind the girl and then at Jacie.

The little girl grinned, then raced over to a nearby tree and picked up an ice cream bucket. She ran back to the girls and held it out to Jacie.

Colored chalk.

Jacie turned to Hannah. "You want me to . . . draw?"

"Of course. You know an international language, Jacie."

Jacie looked at the throng of people nearby. *What if they laugh at me?*

Morgan touched Jacie's arm. "Draw for the kids."

"This is the gift God gave you, Jacie. Use it for His glory," Hannah said.

Lord, help me.

Jacie nodded and carried the bucket to an area away from the path of stomping, shuffling feet. She knelt on the sidewalk and spread color on the smooth cement. The first bold picture to materialize was of Jesus putting children on His lap and loving them. As she continued to draw, her concepts emerged out of vague beginning lines. She breathed silent prayers over the work.

Soon, children squatted around her, chatting happily in Spanish. They touched Jacie and pointed to the pictures.

Jacie portrayed Jesus in many situations with children. At the end of the stream of pictures, she drew Jesus on the cross, the same children surrounding Him. The little ones watching Jacie draw looked up at her confused. She continued drawing—the tomb with people putting Jesus inside. And then, the tomb with Jesus bursting forth from it. *Lord, open their hearts to understand,* Jacie thought. She drew a picture of Jesus embracing the children again. The final picture was of Jesus playing with the children in heaven.

A translator came over and explained each of the pictures to the small army of youngsters. In a large circle, clasping hands with the children, he prayed and they joined in. Jacie listened with her eyes open, watching the eager faces as some gave their hearts, their lives, to Jesus.

"Because of your gift, Jacie."

Thank You, God.

As the team gathered their things to get back on the bus, Jacie felt a tug on her elbow. She looked down to see the little girl whose chalk she'd used.

"Thank you, *gracias*," Jacie said. *Are we supposed to pay her for letting us use the chalk?* she wondered.

The little girl held out the bucket. *"Por favor . . . "*

"I can't draw anymore. We have to leave." Jacie knew the little girl didn't understand her, but she couldn't turn away and board the bus without responding to her. "Morgan, could you come here, please?" she called.

The little girl spoke slowly to Morgan, who turned to Jacie.

"She wants you to keep the chalk. She wants you to draw pictures for other people."

"Meet you by the pool in 10 minutes!" called Corey, racing up the hotel stairs to his room.

"You better give us 15," shouted Celia.

"More like 20," Joelle said.

Jacie grinned. Finally, she'd be able to go swimming with the rest of the group.

"Jacie." Gregg stood in front of her. "Can I talk to you for a minute?"

"Of course." Jacie was relieved that Gregg said something. She'd been meaning to apologize to him all day but never had the chance.

He guided her into a corner of the lobby.

"Gregg, before you say anything, I need to let you know I'm sorry about what I said yesterday. I shouldn't have gone off on you the way I did. Can you forgive me?"

"Sure," Gregg said. "I mean, it really stung and all, but my brother told me that girls can get way overemotional about stuff and say things they don't mean. But we guys can be tough and ignore it. Girls eventually come to their senses."

Jacie bit her lip to keep from arguing. Now wasn't the time to explain that he really could be annoying. "Something like that," she said. "So, what did you want to talk to me about?"

"Well," Gregg took a deep breath. "I wanted to ask you to be my girlfriend."

"What?"

"I know we can't date on the trip, but I thought after we leave, we could be boyfriend and girlfriend."

"Gregg—"

"I know we live far away, but we could call and e-mail. Maybe even visit each other."

Jacie closed her eyes for a second to rein in her frenetic thoughts. "Gregg, I don't think that's a good idea."

"Why?"

Because I can't stand you, she thought. "Well, our age for one thing. We're at completely different stages in our life. At 17, I'm thinking about college, and you're 13—"

"I'm 15." Gregg's eyes clouded. "I'll be 16 in September."

Good move, Jacie.

"Gregg, I think you're a great guy, but I'm not attracted to you in that way." She chose her words carefully. "I can't be your girlfriend."

"Even if I stopped being annoying?" He picked at a scab on his thumb.

"Yes."

He looked up, his eyes bright. "You *could* date me if I was less annoying?"

"No. I couldn't." This was going all wrong. "You're not annoying. I mean some girls would find you really funny, but I—"

"But you don't."

"We just have a different sense of humor," Jacie explained.

"So there's nothing I can do." He went back to picking the scab.

Jacie sat silent.

"I called my parents last night," he said. "I told them I'd met this really cool girl—who likes me. I've never had anyone like me. My dad was like, 'Way to go, Son.' Now I have to tell them I imagined the whole thing. And made a complete moron of myself in the meantime." His voice started to shake.

"There will be other girls, Gregg. You have to believe that. Maybe you need to grow up a little first before the right girl comes along."

"I'll never get there." Gregg ran his fingers through his mop of mousy-brown hair. "Y'know I've never been anywhere where people liked me."

Jacie took in Gregg's lanky arms and legs and hunched posture. She could understand him feeling that way. Truthfully, Gregg was easy to overlook.

"My older brother is super athletic—all the kids like him. My little brother is brilliant—he's all the teachers' favorite. But there's nothing special about me."

Jacie could tell that Gregg was processing many of his feelings out loud for the first time. She kept her mouth shut and listened.

"And when I got here. Everyone was nice to me. Especially you."

"There are a lot of great things about you. You're—"

Gregg cut her off. "I don't need you to think of some way to make me feel better, Jacie. Thanks anyway." And with that, he ran up the stairs.

Oh, God. What did I do now?

● ● ●

Jacie felt like a fish swimming upstream as she fought her way through the hyped-up crowd leaving FUAGNEM.

Lia caught her arm. "Where are you going?! We're serenading the guys tonight, and we need to get upstairs and paint our faces."

Jacie shouted over the crowd, "Go ahead without me. I need some time by myself."

"Are you okay?"

Jacie nodded. She ducked into the bathroom to get away from the stampede. Her back was sticky with sweat, her nose and cheeks shiny. She splashed water on her face, catching sight of herself in the mirror. She stopped to examine the reflection. Her dark brown hair hung in limp curls against her damp face. Half circles spread under her eyes, dark even compared to her quick-tanning complexion. The color of her skin could almost be considered Venezuelan, she noticed. In Miami, they'd been told to be careful because Venezuelan men are fascinated by fair American girls. With shimmery blonde hair and cornflower blue eyes, Hannah certainly had received her share of attention, as had other girls on the team. But Jacie hadn't—not that she wanted that kind of unnerving flirtation—but it made her feel she wasn't special here either.

She opened the bathroom door and slipped out. She hadn't bothered to dry her face. There weren't paper towels anyway. She moved along the hallway and out into the patio where the evening meeting had been held. A few stragglers chatted in groups. Ten minutes until room curfew when she'd have to face the happy chatter and questions of her friends. But she'd use every minute she had left to evade them. She needed to think. She needed to figure out how to apologize to Gregg. How to sort things out with Corey. To pray for Jared.

A cool evening breeze sifted through the leaves above her, and the scent of magnolia wafted down. She wished she could hide in the darkness. Hide permanently from the world. She sighed. The entire day hadn't been a waste. It had a few hopeful moments. She felt incredibly alive while drawing for the children. Purpose, joy, and passion filled her as the chalk squeaked across the pavement. But flanking that were horrible conversations—one with Jared and two with Gregg. She cringed at the memories. She had been hurtful, pointless, and stupid. *I'm a dangerous person*, she thought. *Everywhere I go, I'm a mud slide leaving a trail of devastation behind me.* Jared trusted her enough to share his deepest pain with her, and she gave him nothing in return. Gregg found a place where he felt loved and accepted, and she'd pretty much crushed his hopes and told him he was annoying. Corey still thought she was a flake and a flirt. And who knew what the rest of the team thought?

I don't want to be this person. I don't want to be afraid. I don't want to be quiet. I don't want to be useless. I don't want to hurt people.

"Jacie," Berk's voice punctured the stillness. "Are you out here?"

Before Jacie could decide whether to say anything, he noticed her.

"There you are! I've been looking everywhere for you," he said.

"Why?"

"I wanted to talk to you about something."

"Do you want me to go home?"

"No! Of course not. Why would you say such a thing?"

"I've just kind of made a mess of things."

"You mean with Gregg."

Jacie nodded. "Yeah, and not just him."

"I only know about Gregg," Berk continued. "He told me about what happened. But that wasn't your fault—he knows that."

Jacie stared down at her hands. "I just feel like I've done a whole lot more harm here than good."

"That's not true."

Jacie smirked. "Yeah, right."

"You're friends with everyone. Because of your example and friendliness, we haven't split off into cliques."

Jacie looked skeptical.

"And you're an incredible artist. Today the kids flocked to see your drawings and give you hugs. And even if you didn't do those things, you'd still be amazing. Because you're Jacie. You're funny and loving and sunshiny and have an amazingly beautiful heart. You listen to girls pour out their hearts, and you respond with genuine compassion."

A lump rose in her throat. She swallowed it back. "Thanks for thinking that, Berk, but I don't see what you see."

"I wish you did. I can't make you see it or believe it. I only know it's true," he said. Berk leaned forward, his elbows pressing against his knees. "Jacie, I don't know your whole story. But you are a beautiful young lady, and you deserve someone in your life who reminds you of that." He paused for a moment as though contemplating a thought. "I hope your dad appreciates the young woman he has."

"My dad lives far away. I don't see him much."

"He's missing out." Berk gently tilted her chin up to make eye contact. "He's missing out on something really good."

Tears flowed freely down Jacie's face, and Berk wrapped a big arm around her. "You're a wonderful daughter."

Something in Jacie shattered like glass—crumbling into a pile of razor-sharp shards.

"No, I'm not. If I was, my father would want to be with me. He would have come to my middle-school graduation. He would call to see how I did on my finals. He wouldn't live so far away. I'm so mad at him for that—and for so much more," she said through her sobs, her nose running as much as her eyes. "And I'm hurt that he got me a briefcase for Christmas.

"Oh, Berk, I want my daddy to love me, to protect me, to be there. He tries. I know he does. It must be so hard to be a parent from a distance. So why isn't his trying enough for me? What an incredibly selfish person I am to want more."

She swiped her nose with the back of her arm and looked straight at Berk. "I'm sorry that now you know I'm not a wonderful daughter. I'm a selfish, snotty kid."

Berk wrapped his arms around her, letting her sob. Then he pulled back, lifting her chin. "No you're not. And you deserve so much more than what your dad has given to you."

"He's not a bad dad, he's just . . ." She didn't know how to say it.

"Not around?"

Jacie nodded. The lump in her throat didn't allow anything else. Why did she have to cry about everything?

Berk leaned in closer. "It's okay that you want your dad to be a close, integral part of your life. It's okay to want hugs and compliments and protection from him."

No it's not, she wanted to say. *Because wishing only brings disappointment.* She remembered searching the middle-school graduation crowd for his bold smile, thinking, *There's no way he would miss this. I bet he's planning to surprise me.* But he wasn't there.

I hate being disappointed. I hate wanting things I can't have.

"God created you to have those desires," Berk was saying.

Jacie looked up and squeaked her voice past the lump. "If that's the way God wanted it, then why don't I have it?"

Berk shook his head. "I don't know. We live in a fallen world, and sin messes up the way God originally designed things to be."

"Great. So what hope is there?"

Berk met Jacie's eyes in a way that forced her to continue looking at him. "Oh, Jacie. There's so much hope. God says He will be a Father to the fatherless. He'll provide you with the love and protection and encouragement you need. He wants to do that for you."

Jacie jumped up, blood rushing to her face. She'd heard that platitude before. It made her angry. At her dad, at God, and at Berk. "Oh sure, Berk. Everything is supposed to be okay because 'God loves me.' But things aren't okay, and I'm not sure God loves me. How do I know He really cares? How can He be my father? He doesn't bring home a paycheck when bills are tight. He doesn't hug me when I have a rotten day, or laugh with me when I'm in a silly mood. HE'S NOT HERE. I can't see Him. I can't touch Him. It's not the same as having a human dad."

"I know it's not the same. That's why God wanted human dads in the picture. But when your dad steps out, He steps in. Think about it. He's always provided, hasn't He? He's put people in your life to love you and encourage you. And He's been there through them. Do you ever feel it?"

Jacie leaned against the stone wall, slowly breathing in the scents of the night and allowing them to clear her head. She knew it was true. She had friends who hugged her. Teachers who encouraged her. Men in her life she respected—Becca's dad, her teacher Mr. Garner, and Berk. Even when things were tight financially, she and her mom always had enough—barely, but enough. Even when she was scared, God was with her. And, yes, when she sat cross-legged on her bed at night in silence, there were moments she felt His presence. Maybe He was there—watching, waiting, even . . . loving.

"I believe God can be a Father if you let Him, Jacie. If you ask Him to be. Every time you wish your dad was there, call out to God and ask Him to take your dad's place. He'll do it, and He might just do a better job."

"Do you really think so?" she asked, desperately wanting something to fill the ache inside.

"Yes I do. And I think He is reaching out to you. You just need to take the step of faith and reach up. Trust Him, Jacie, even when it's hard."

Reach up. She remembered the feelings she experienced during worship time the last couple weeks. It felt like God reaching out to her, wanting to speak to her, wanting to love her. "I want to reach up," she said softly. "But I don't know how."

Berk smiled. "Just ask, Jacie. Picture yourself asking God if you can crawl into His lap so He can be your Daddy."

Jacie bit her bottom lip. *Could it really happen?*

"I have another question for you," Berk said.

Jacie focused her attention back on the team leader.

"Who chose your name?"

Talk about changing gears! "My mom."

"How did she choose it?"

Jacie smiled. She asked for the story many times when she was little. "She was going to name me Amber, but then, when they placed me in her arms, she looked at me and knew I wasn't an Amber. 'Jacie' popped into her head, and she knew that's who I was."

"I think God named you, whispering your name into your mom's ear." Berk touched Jacie's arm with his strong hand. "Jacie means 'beautiful one,' and I believe that's what you are to God."

Beautiful one?

"You were never an accident, Jacie. You were born to be God's daughter."

Mom said, "It just came to mind when I saw your face."

Berk watched her.

Beautiful one.

She breathed in the magnolias. She watched the flickering of the city lights.

A God who planned my birth, knowing I'd live in a single-parent home, knowing my dad didn't want kids, yet designing me anyway? A God who named me and who wants to be my Dad? Maybe . . . maybe that was a God she could trust. "Berk?"

"Yes, Jacie."

"Do you still have that bond servant necklace?"

chapter 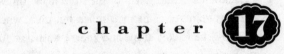 17

This trip is so not what I expected it to be. Sure, there have been moments of fun, especially last night. We laughed so much that my stomach is sore today. But I didn't come on the trip to have fun. I came to do serious work. I'm discouraged. I keep thinking about what Susie said—that sacrifice doesn't matter, our obedience does. I'm trying to be obedient, but at this point I don't even know what that looks like.

"Okay, everyone, hold on!" Corey called. He pushed a button and immediately, the entire bus gyrated with blaring Christian pop music.

"What do you mean 'hold on'?" shouted Lia over the funky beat. "I'm getting up and gettin' down."

She stood up in the aisle and started practicing her '70s dance moves.

"Woo-hoo," shouted Corey. "It's Team 10's own Joan Travolta."

"I'm stayin' alive," she yelled back.

"Go Lia. Go Lia," the rest of the bus chanted, clapping to the beat of the music.

Lia pulled Jacie out of the seat behind her, and the two started jiving. Soon Morgan, Celia, and Laurilee surrounded them, arms in the air, hips swinging. Even Berk and Melanie joined the rest of the bus singing along.

Phoebe and others started their own version of line dancing in the back of the bus—a little difficult to do in an 18-inch aisle.

Hannah underlined "I came to do serious work" in her journal. She thought the team should be praying or practicing with their cards or *something*. Mercedes tripped while line dancing and fell into Gregg's lap. She shrieked in surprise—and so did Gregg. Laughter came from everyone on the bus, including Hannah. Catching herself, she cleared her throat. As the third song ended, Hannah called over the fading chords, "Shouldn't we turn off the music and pray? We're going to be performing pretty soon." The moment the words came out of her mouth, she wanted to stuff them back. Even the quieter kids in the front of the bus turned to shoot glares at her. *But this is what You'd want us to do. Right, God?*

"R-i-i-i-g-h-t," Corey said. "How about after the next song?" He turned up the stereo, and the party resumed.

"C'mon, Hannah." Joelle tugged at Hannah's long arms. "Get up here and show us your stuff."

"I don't think so. I'm not much of a dancer."

"Sure you are. Here, just follow Mercedes and Phoebe."

Phoebe grinned. "How 'bout the Macarena? You know that, right?"

Hannah shook her head. She watched their arms move in unison—from hips to shoulders to heads. She'd never felt so awkward in her life.

She tried to follow but always seemed to be elbowing someone in the face. Everyone else gently swayed their hips, and she felt stiff as a board. She breathed a sigh of relief as the song came to a close and Corey shut off the stereo.

"Okay, Hannah, go for it," Corey said.

By the time Hannah finished praying about the performance, the bus rolled up to a curb.

"Amen," cited a chorus of voices. The bus door opened with a hiss.

Corey repacked the stereo and speakers into the silver trunk and slid it off the bus. The rest of the team bustled to locate props and touch up makeup.

Melanie's voice projected over the flurry, "Okay, everyone! We only have two more performance days left. So let's make the most of this."

● ● ●

Their two performances in blistering heat had been exhausting. The bus lurched, jarring Hannah awake. She sat up, stretching. Glancing at her watch, she realized she'd been asleep for at least half an hour. She leaned her weary head against the window, watching the city move by. She watched the people walk by and thought about the day.

She recalled talking with a middle-aged couple—Pablo and Maria—after their last performance. Maria was in a wheelchair, her salt-and-pepper hair pulled back in a thick bun. Pablo clearly doted on her. They spoke little bits of English, and the three somehow pieced together a semblance of a conversation—about the United States, the weather, and the couple's children. Despite Hannah's many attempts to bring Jesus up in the conversation, neither had an interest in hearing about Him.

"Team 10!" Melanie called from the front of the bus. "We'll be stopping momentarily at McDonald's. What do you think? Is it okay if we eat at Mickey D's instead of the hotel?"

The bus erupted in cheers.

"Are we going to get back in time for FUAGNEM?" Hannah asked, sounding half asleep.

For some reason, Melanie choked back a laugh. "Yep. We'll have plenty of time." She sat down and then stood up again. "Don't forget to take advantage of McDonald's nice restrooms."

"Looks like we weren't the only team with this idea," Berk said, pointing at two other busses and crowds of kids milling about the outside eating area.

"Great!"

"Yeah!"

"Oh, look! There's Jen!"

Team 10 poured out of the bus and invaded the restaurant, creating a snake-like line extending out the door.

"Bathrooms!" said Celia, pushing through the crowd. "Clean ones."

"Hot water!" Mercedes shouted.

"I never thought something so simple could bring me such joy," giggled April.

It seemed most of the kids headed for the restrooms, so Hannah decided to wait until later. Besides, her growling stomach was most insistent.

Kylie and Valerie talked behind her in line.

"Wasn't that amazing? Praying with an entire family!" Valerie was saying.

"They were so eager. I've never experienced anything like it," Kylie said. "And did you see the mom? She had tears streaming down her face the entire time we were praying."

Hannah quickly placed her order, pointing to the value meal she wanted. "*Gracias*," she kept saying. Since "*gracias*" was one of the only words she knew, she'd have said it even if they had given her an empty paper bag. She took her receipt and grabbed her dinner while trying not to hear the two girls talking. But Valerie's high voice couldn't be ignored.

155

"I can't believe I was so scared of sharing my faith while we were in Miami. It's been a lot easier than I expected."

I need some fresh air. Hannah sidestepped the rest of the line and shoved open the glass door. She breathed in the cool break from another hot day. Light still hung in the evening air, and Hannah admired the pink-painted mountains in the distance. *God, if You can make a scene like that, why can't You help me lead someone to salvation?*

Hannah stepped back as a bedraggled man shuffled across the parking lot about 15 feet from where she stood. A long graying beard covered his gaunt face. Bushy brows peeked out over downcast eyes. The sole of his shoe flopped along the asphalt, creating a slapping sound with each step. He didn't notice her watching him. He stuck his hand in a nearby trash can and rummaged through the contents. He pulled out a brown paper McDonald's bag and picked through it. Hannah's heart dropped as the man pulled out a few fries and crammed them in his mouth. *He must be so hungry.* She ran up to him and held out her bag. He stared at her, confused.

"For you," she said. She picked up his hand hanging at his side and placed the bag in it. He slowly opened it and looked inside, closing his eyes as the scent of fresh hamburger escaped.

"*Gracias, Señorita,*" he said. Hannah noticed tears in his worn eyes but a big smile spread across his wrinkled face.

If only I knew what to say, Hannah thought. *If only I knew a little Spanish.* "God loves you," she stammered. The man nodded, obviously more absorbed in his meal. He thanked her once again, then turned to leave. *Flop, flop, flop,* the sole of his shoe smacked until Hannah lost sight of him.

She reentered the restaurant, hungrier than ever, but wishing she'd known something else to say to the man. *If only I'd thought to take Morgan with me. It could've been such a perfect opportunity to share the gospel.* She felt a hand touch her arm.

"Well, look at you!" an exuberant voice said.

Hannah swung around at the sound of it.

"Look who I found!" Jacie said happily, her arms linked through Becca's and Tyler's.

Becca threw her arms around Hannah. "It's so good to see you! How's it goin'? How many zillions of people have you talked to?"

Hannah took a deep breath, not wanting to confess her failures.

Tyler saved her. "You've been, well, you've been . . . look at you!"

"Look at you?" Hannah echoed, confused.

Jacie's smile was all twisted up on her face.

"Tell you what," Becca said, looking curiously at Jacie, then back at Hannah. "Why don't you go wash up, and I'll get your dinner."

"I can—"

"Go!" Tyler ordered, pointing toward the restrooms.

Baffled, Hannah moved toward the restroom. As she pushed on the door, she heard her friends break into laughter.

She stepped into the room and turned on the tap. Looking into the mirror, she froze. *Oh, no.* Under her slipping tiara princess prop and disheveled hair, someone had drawn glasses around her eyes in bright red lipstick. They had used a black eye pencil to give her a smart mustache and bushy eyebrows.

Note to self: Never fall asleep on a bus of teenagers with makeup.

● ● ●

"I must've looked like a complete idiot to that homeless man," bemoaned Hannah, banging her head against the bus window.

Melanie sat next to her. Hannah had decided the leader reminded her a little of her mom. Casual, nurturing, energetic. She was easy to talk with, and her response sounded like the mom-thing to say: "I don't think he cared at all what you looked like. He was hungry and you gave him food. He probably just thought you were a strange-looking angel."

"Why can't one thing go right?" Hannah said. "Why can't I lead one person to the Lord? Why can't I show God's love once without looking like a moron? Why do I have to be the only person on the team to fail?"

Melanie took a deep breath. "Can I tell you a story?"

Hannah raised her eyebrows.

"It's about me."

"Sure." She tried to sound enthused.

"When I was in high school, I ran for student council. I prayed and prayed that God would allow me to get elected so I could have a positive Christian influence on the school."

"I did that too," Hannah butted in. "Well, sort of. That's why I joined the school newspaper."

Melanie nodded. "And I knew God wanted this for me."

"Of course," Hannah agreed. *Maybe she's trying to tell me to persevere, even while things don't look promising.*

"My whole youth group was praying for me. We knew God would want a Christian in a leadership position. I was confident God would place me in that position."

"Faith," Hannah noted. *Maybe that's what I need more of.*

"On election day, I waited and prayed with my friends. People told me not to get my hopes up, but, like you said, I had faith. And I wasn't giving up for anything. I believed. Then, right before the final bell rang, the announcement came." Melanie paused. "And I lost."

Hannah's eyes widened. *That wasn't the way the story was supposed to go.* "Why?"

"I had no idea," Melanie said. "I trusted God. I prayed. I'd been faithful. I openly shared my faith."

Exactly, Hannah thought.

"But then something funny happened." Melanie touched Hannah's arm. "The girl who ran against me called a month later. Liz had just found out her mom had cancer, and because she knew I was a Christian, she asked me to pray for her mom. The two of us began to spend more time together and, a few weeks later, Liz believed in Jesus."

"That's awesome," Hannah said.

"But it gets better. Together, we started a Bible study in our public school, which grew to over 200 kids before I graduated. And it was something I never would have had time for if I was on student council. I realized God had used me to impact my school in an incredible way. And in a way I'd never expected."

"Did you ask God if He wanted you on student council?"

"I did, but I don't know if I ever really listened to the answer. I think I just assumed this would be a good thing for the kingdom, so, of course, God would want this. But God had His own plan. It was different than my original idea, but in the end it was far greater."

"What an amazing story," Hannah said. "That's the kind of thing I wish I could tell people about this trip when I get home."

Melanie shook her head as though Hannah didn't get her point. "Do you know Jeremiah 29:11, Hannah?"

"Of course. 'I know the plans I have for you. Plans to prosper you and not to harm you. Plans to give you hope and a future,' " she quoted.

Melanie raised her eyebrows. "It says 'God knows the plans' not 'Hannah knows the plans.' Maybe His plans aren't quite what you think. The truth is, His plans are better than ours could ever be."

● ● ●

Hannah moved through the crowd that spilled into the patio area.

"You'll want front-row seats for this one, guys and gals," Susie said from the stage. "We are gonna be jammin' tonight!"

Susie did her not-so-great moon walk off stage, and several of the kids cheered her on for more.

Joelle took a last swig of milk. "Let's get good seats tonight. I love our worship."

"It's been awesome," agreed Morgan, wiping her mouth with a napkin. "It's funny. I don't really enjoy worship at church, but here it just seems so real—so alive."

"All this praise keeps pourin' outta me. I'm just jumpin' around out of this joy inside for God an' all," said Laurilee.

"It actually makes me excited about heaven," said Jacie.

"No joke," nodded Morgan. "I used to think heaven would be boring, but now, I'm thinking it's going to be a blast."

Hannah tugged at a braid. She wasn't having the same experience as her friends. She desired God's presence. But she didn't feel like she'd earned it. Everyone else was using their gifts and bringing people into a relationship with God. Why would God want to give to her when she wasn't giving anything back? *But I'm trying, God. I'm trying.*

Four hundred teenagers jumped to their feet, cheering when Susie introduced the famous Christian musicians who climbed the stairs to the stage.

"Let's worship!" the lead singer called out.

The first song was one of Hannah's favorites—but she'd never heard it live before. She let the music flow through her. She swayed with the rest of the crowd and sang along with the chorus.

In between sets the singers talked about their faith and what they'd been learning in the Word. Hannah was impressed. They really knew God and desired a strong relationship with Him. This wasn't about a performance or getting glory for themselves. Their purpose was clearly to show God's love to others.

A lively drum intro caused the audience to erupt, and the group on stage broke out into choreographed dance moves. Like waves in the ocean, the audience jumped in time with the beat. A conga line started snaking through the crowd, and Jacie grabbed Hannah by the hand.

"Come on, Hannah," she called over the pulsing music. "Latch on!" Several other girls from the team attached themselves behind Jacie.

Hannah reached out, grabbed the last person's waist in line, and found herself being pulled through the crowd like a long strand of spaghetti in boiling water.

She sang and shouted and laughed. And somewhere in her, deep down, she knew God was smiling.

chapter

Clouds meandered across the sky, providing a welcome coolness from the sun. Performing as the Clown was becoming more natural and less nerve-racking. But Jacie's heart still beat fast when the invitation was given. What if someone approached her with questions? What would she say?

"We've only got a couple days left, gang," Berk announced in a raspy voice from the side of the stage. Projecting his voice for two weeks had taken its toll. "Let's make the most of it."

Team 10 whooped and headed out into the crowd.

Jacie surveyed the scene and headed to the pile of backpacks to stand guard.

"Nuh-uh." Lia stepped in front of her, arms crossed. "You grab your bucket of chalk and get to work, young lady. You've got drawing to do."

Jacie laughed and fingered her bond servant necklace. She knew she didn't need to be shy or afraid. Her dad had given her the ability to draw. "Yes, Ma'am," she said, saluting her friend.

A group of wide-eyed children soon surrounded her, watching her arm move across the sidewalk leaving bold, colorful illustrations behind. A little boy squatted next to her, chatting animatedly with his little brother, pointing at the picture of Jesus.

"*Jesus!*" The little brother said in Spanish, grinning up at Jacie.

"*Sí,*" Jacie nodded. "*Jesus.*"

She looked up to relieve the crick in her neck and noticed Hannah near a tree talking with two older women. She had her laminated card out in front of her, and she waved her arms about vigorously. The women looked at each other and then back at Hannah. They shook their heads and chuckled, then began to walk away. Hannah stepped in front of them and said something else. The women stepped around her.

The little boy beside Jacie pulled on the sleeve of her T-shirt. "*Dibuje, por favor.*" He pointed at the unfinished art, bringing Jacie back to the task at her knees.

● ● ●

"Those pictures were amazing, Jacie." Corey slid onto the green vinyl bus seat next to Jacie. "You're an awesome artist."

"I hope I will be someday," Jacie said, feeling her cheeks grow warm.

"Look!" He pointed out the window as the bus lurched forward. "That little girl is explaining the pictures to her friend."

"Wow." Jacie shook her head. "It's amazing how God uses things."

"Awwww." Phoebe's groan came from the back of the bus. "Mega-bummer. It's starting to rain."

Sure enough, fat drops of rain splatted against the bus windows. Some kids hung their hands and faces outside the casements, catching the cool water on sweaty skin.

"It's going to ruin Jacie's artwork," said Valerie.

"It's raining on the bread!" Kylie gasped and dove to close a window. "Gross. I hate soggy bread."

"Don't we have another performance today, Melanie?" Joelle shouted.

"I don't like peanut butter and jelly sandwiches anyway," Kylie mumbled to herself. "Jelly makes me nauseous."

Melanie, sitting in the front seat, twisted around to face the group. "Yes we do. But if the rain keeps up, we'll probably head back to the hotel."

"Yeah," agreed Celia. "No one's going to watch if it's storming."

"I'm more than a little tuckered out," said Laurilee. "Turning in early sounds just fine with me."

Jacie closed her eyes, thinking how nice it would be to lounge around, or maybe catch up on some sleep. The lingering cough still kept her from feeling 100 percent.

Other comments bounced around the bus. After nine performances in three days, evening meetings, and late-night talks, everyone looked exhausted.

"What do you mean?" Kylie's whining voice spoke up. "We can't quit."

"You said just this morning you thought you might be getting sick," April reminded her.

"Don't listen to Kylie. She just needs something to complain about," said Gregg.

"That's not true!" Kylie stood up, hands on her hips. "Well, maybe it is. Maybe I do complain a lot, but—well, to be totally honest—I like the way it feels to be out there doing what I really think God wants me to do."

The bus fell quiet.

Kylie bit her lip. "How can we let a little rain keep us from performing? If God wants people there, then they'll be there. Susie said on our first day that God is the one who changes hearts. We only need to be available. But giving up isn't being available."

Joelle spoke up, "So you're saying we should go out there even though our makeup will run and our costumes will get waterlogged and we probably won't even get much of an audience."

Kylie paused. "Yes. That's what I'm saying."

Silence.

"Then let's go for it!" Joelle said.

"Yeah!" the bus roared.

Jacie sat at the kitchenette table, combing out her drenched curls. The rained-on performance had a surprisingly good turnout—people congregated under trees to watch and even stayed to talk with the performers afterward. Chalk drawing would have, of course, been futile, so Jacie volunteered to watch bags. But for the first time she didn't feel the least bit left out. After the crowd left, she jumped in mud puddles and danced in the rain with the rest of the team for 20 minutes. Jacie couldn't remember when she'd laughed so hard.

"What are you smiling about?" asked Lia, dropping into a chair. "Or are you just struck by how blessed you are to be in my presence?"

"Something like that," giggled Jacie. "I was remembering how fun it was to play in the rain today. I haven't done that since I was a little kid."

"Yeah," Lia said. "I haven't done it since . . . two weeks ago Tuesday."

The front door slammed. "I need a stamp! I need a stamp, y'all!" Laurilee rushed around the room waving an envelope. "Hurry!"

Jacie peered around the corner of the kitchenette to see what had caused the laid-back Southerner to go into hyperdrive.

Nichole handed her a stamp. "Who's the letter to?"

"Todd. And I need to mail it right now."

"What's the rush?" Jill asked. "You're going to see him in less than a week. You'll beat the letter home anyway."

"I know, but I need to send it while I still have the nerve." She held the envelope up. "In this letter, I explained why he and I need to break up. The thing is, I'm writin' the letter now so I can't chicken out when I see him. Once this gets mailed, I have to go through with it. Y'all get it?"

"You've got guts, girl," said Nichole. "Way to be."

The girls took turns hugging her. "We're so proud of you," they told her.

"But y'all can't abandon me. I'll need to call y'all and have you remind me why I did this in the first place."

"You can call anytime," Joelle said, swinging her arm around Lauri-lee's shoulders. "C'mon, I'll go downstairs with you to mail it. I'll be the witness that it was sent."

"That's mega-hard," Phoebe said after the door shut behind them.

"Why don't we set up an e-mail network for all of us to encourage each other?" Jacie said.

"That's a great idea, Jacie," said Celia. "I wish I could take everyone with me. Actually, Corey would make a great souvenir."

"Speaking of souvenirs, I can't wait to go shopping on Saturday," said Jill.

"Me, too," said Lia, folding her legs under her. "But what do you get to remind yourself of the change in your heart?"

"I wish I had something from the devastation that we cleaned up, to remind me how blessed we are," Mercedes added.

"But at least you have that journal," April said to Hannah.

"What journal?" Jacie asked.

"Oh, yeah," Hannah said. "I forgot to tell you. When we were digging out a house one of the days you were sick, I came across a journal that looked a lot like mine. I couldn't bear to dump it with the rest of the rubble."

"Just like you, Hannah, to read someone else's diary," Lia teased.

"I can't even understand Spanish, much less read it."

"You kept that? Cool. We should pull it out and see what it says," Morgan suggested.

Hannah shook her head. "I don't think you'll be able to read anything. The mud ruined most of it."

"Let's just see. I'm curious," Mercedes urged.

Hannah padded into the living room a minute later with the bedraggled journal in hand. "Most of the pages are stuck together, and it's not very legible."

Mercedes gently separated a few pages. "I can read what looks like the last entry. Look at the date, Morgan."

Morgan peered closer. "That's the day of the mud slides."

Phoebe shuddered. "This is mega-freaky."

"Most of it's water-stained," Mercedes said, skimming the page with her finger. She handed the book to Morgan. "You try it. You're better at reading Spanish."

"I can only make out some words. I still love . . . someone. I forgive him. I can't read the next line. I think it's about someone named Angela. She asks God for help—a lot of help. She knows . . . no, that can't be right. Mercedes, what does '*oso*' mean?"

"I think it means 'bear,' " said Mercedes.

Bear. It can't be.

"I thought so, too. But this doesn't make sense. 'I know bear still cares for me'?" Morgan looked up quizzically.

Jacie squeezed in next to Morgan. "Can I see?"

Oh, God . . . The team was digging out Marisa's house.

"Give me that," Jacie said.

"Why?" asked Hannah.

"I need it. I need it now." She grabbed the book and stared at it. She opened it to the front. She could barely make out the writing: *Maris—*

Her heart flipped wildly inside her. "I—someone needs to see this."

Oh, God. Help me get this to Jared.

chapter **19**

At the end of the performance, the Baseball Player, Prince, and a crew of others made their way out into the crowd of Venezuelans. But the Princess held back.

God, it's the last performance. My last chance.

Colorful groups of people gathered in small circles—chattering, laughing. Little hands grabbed for the stickers Morgan and Jill were handing out.

You say that You know the plans You have for me. I only want Your plan, God.

An elderly lady bowed her head to pray with Mercedes.

Help me see Your plan.

The translator held out a Bible for a teenage girl to read. Corey and Lia talked to her a mile a minute. The girl looked teary.

I don't know what You're doing, God. But I want to be obedient and let You be God.

Hannah turned to where Jacie stood by the pile of bags. "I'll watch the bags if it's okay with you."

Jacie looked at Hannah, a crease in her forehead. "You don't need to do that. I know you like to be out in the crowd."

Hannah shook her head. "No, I want to be here."

"Really. It's my job. I can do it."

"I thought I came to Venezuela to be a great evangelist, but apparently that's not what God had in mind. I'm just here to serve. And right now that means watching the packs."

"But—" began Jacie.

"Jacie, your chalk drawings are impacting people more than anything I can do right now."

Jacie stared at her.

Hannah assured her, "Okay?"

"Okay. Thanks, Hannah." Jacie unzipped her pack, dug out the bucket of chalk, and scampered off to find an open place on the ground.

Hannah hoisted herself up onto a cement wall, her gaze sweeping over the mound of backpacks. *Well, God, no one's going to steal a pack while I'm watching.*

"*Hola,*" came a young voice next to her. Hannah glanced down to see a little girl. *She looks like she's Rebekah's age.* Hannah pictured her 10-year-old sister. She loved to wear her hair in two pigtails just like this little girl.

"*Hola,*" Hannah replied.

The little girl giggled. She pointed one chubby finger at her chest. "Maria." She pointed the same finger at Hannah. "Princess."

Hannah grinned. The little girl knew some English. She pointed her own finger at herself and said, "Hannah."

Together, intermingling bits of Spanish and English with lots of pantomime, the two managed to communicate tidbits of information about family, school, and things Maria liked to do.

"Do you go to church?" Hannah asked slowly, trying to form one out of her hands.

"*Iglesia?*" The girl's brown eyes looked down. "No."

"Do you know Jesus?" Hannah continued to prod.

The little girl looked up again, searching Hannah's face. "No."

"Can I help?" a deep voice with a thick Spanish accent asked.

Hannah looked up to see Felipe, one of their interpreters. "Yes!" she said.

The young man introduced himself to Maria. The little girl said something back.

Felipe turned to Hannah. "She says she liked the play but doesn't think Jesus would come choose her to dance with Him like He did with the other toys."

"Ask her why," Hannah responded.

The two talked for a moment, and Hannah saw the girl's eyes brim with tears.

Felipe turned to her again. "She said she was like you in the play. She's been mean to other people—including her little brothers and sisters. She's been too bad for Jesus to love her."

"Of course He can. He does!" Forgetting momentarily Maria couldn't understand her very well, Hannah jumped down from her perch, put one hand on each of the child's shoulders, and looked into her eyes. "Maria, God loves you very much. That's why He created you. Jesus came to forgive you for your sins. Of course God can forgive you. He wants to forgive you more than anything."

Felipe rushed his words to keep up with Hannah's. And Maria responded with the same fervor. Hannah felt her heart pour out on Maria. The child's heart was so precious, so loving, so wanting God. Hannah felt a sense of how much God must love this little girl. That love rushed out to meet Maria.

Hannah shared from her own life, how even though she was still disobedient many times, God continued to forgive her. Maria seemed to find comfort in this, but she still had more questions. How could she know Jesus died for her and not just everyone else? How many times would Jesus forgive her? Perspiration formed on Felipe's forehead as he attempted to keep up with Hannah's replies.

A light went on inside Maria, and she grasped Hannah's hand. "*Quisiera conocer a Jesus.*"

Felipe asked Maria a question in Spanish and then said, "She wants you to pray with her. She wants to talk to Jesus."

Tears involuntarily sprung from Hannah's eyes as she continued to hold tightly to Maria's trembling hands.

"O . . . okay," Hannah stammered.

"Okay," Maria grinned.

Hannah bowed her head and prayed out loud for Maria.

"God, this precious girl wants You to love her. And we know You already do. Will You please let her feel Your love? And would You help her to hear Your voice today and always?"

Then Maria prayed in Spanish, with Felipe's soft voice translating.

"Jesus, I want You," Maria said in Spanish. "Do You want me? Princess Hannah says that You love me even though I've done so many bad things. She says that it will be like You giving me a bath and washing away all the bad things I've done. Will You do that? I would be so happy if You would. And she says that You will keep giving me baths when I do bad things again. Please don't ever go away. I want to be with You always. Amen."

"Amen," said Hannah.

"Amen," said Felipe.

Maria lunged into Hannah's arms and gave her a tight squeeze. Hannah leaned down and kissed the girl's cheek.

Suddenly she remembered the bags but was relieved to see Berk guarding the pile. Well, what was left of the pile at least.

"Almost everyone is on the bus, Hannah," he said. "We need to get going."

How can we leave now? Maria had just stepped from one world and into another. How could Hannah just ride off on a bus? Someone had to guide Maria, disciple her.

Felipe must have read her mind. "We'll get Maria connected with a church. She said she lives in this area, and I go to a great church down the block."

"Will you take her if she needs someone to go with?" Hannah asked.

"Absolutely," Felipe said. Hannah knew she could trust him.

"Tell her to wait a minute," she said, grabbing her backpack.

She unzipped it and pulled out her treasured Bible. Her parents had presented it to her on her 10th birthday. She had underlined in it and taken tons of notes on the side, but she so badly wanted something for Maria to remember her by. And she didn't have to give it a second thought.

She yanked her pen out of the side pocket and opened the front cover.

> *Maria,*
>
> *Stay close to Jesus. I'll be praying for you. I can't wait to see you again in heaven.*
>
> *Love,*
> *your sister in Christ,*
> *Hannah*

She placed the Bible in Maria's hands.

Maria gave Hannah a long hug. "*Gracias, mi amiga.*"

● ● ●

"I can't believe it's over." Hannah slid into the seat next to Jacie as the bus lurched away from the curb. "The last performance."

"I know. Although, I have to admit, going to the beach tomorrow sounds pretty good," said Jacie, her eyes closed.

"Yeah, it does."

Jacie's eyes popped open. "So you're okay with slacking for a day at the beach instead of doing ministry?"

"I think God is okay with us taking a day off," Hannah said decidedly.

Jacie stood back, inspecting Hannah.

"What?" Hannah asked. "Hey. Even God took one day to take a rest. Besides, we could probably bring our costumes and set up the sound system on the beach. Jacie, we could fit in two or three performances in the time we're there—" Hannah grinned and elbowed Jacie.

Jacie shook her head and closed her eyes again. "Hannah, I'm sleeping. I'm not listening."

But it was at that moment that Corey decided it was time to hit the music to begin another dance session, ending any ideas of sleep or conversation.

● ● ●

The sun warmed Hannah's back. She loved the sound of the waves crashing onto the shore. She lay her head on her thick blue beach towel. Phoebe, Jacie, Laurilee, Joelle, and Lia surrounded her. The girls' bodies made a sort of giant wheel—their heads in the middle and their legs like spokes coming out of the center. Hannah dozed in and out, half-listening to the chatter surrounding her.

"I think the event that changed me the most was the FUAGNEM where Susie talked about God wanting to heal us," Phoebe said. "When I sat in that wheelchair with all of you surrounding me, I was blown away by your love and prayers—it was mega-incredible."

"I loved that night too," agreed Laurilee. "I put the Band-Aid I got in my journal as a reminder. But my best moment was mailing that letter."

"Chalk drawings," Jacie said. "The bond servant necklace, starting to see how God can really be my Dad."

"Ooga-Booga Club. Decorating Hannah's face on the bus," Joelle said. "Talking until late every night with you guys and getting to know your hearts."

"I have too many memories," Lia said. "I'm glad I took gobs of pictures of everything. I think I even have some great ones of you doing your chalk drawings, Jacie. I'll send you the doubles."

"Thanks," said Jacie.

"Hannah, what was your favorite part of the trip?" Joelle asked.

Hannah lifted her head and rested it on two stacked fists. "The best part was talking with Maria. The hardest part was the arguing I did with God."

"You? Argue with God?" Jacie sounded surprised.

Hannah gave her a half smile.

"Did He want you to wear stripes and plaids together? I always get that from Him."

The girls turned to look at Lia.

"Well, at least that's my excuse when I don't match."

Hannah stared up at the wisps of clouds overhead. "Maybe I shouldn't call it arguing, but I really struggled with what God wanted from me these past couple weeks."

"It seemed to me you were giving Him your all," Joelle said.

"I was," Hannah said slowly. "But I was giving Him everything on my terms. I just wanted to be—" Hannah sighed. She put her forehead onto her fists. "I'm ashamed to say I wanted to be a superstar for God. I wanted everyone to say what a great Christian I was. What a great evangelist. That I was the perfect Christian girl. I wanted to be the best at everything."

No one said anything. Hannah finally looked up at them. Instead of disgust, she saw compassion and understanding on their faces.

"What do you think God wanted?" Phoebe finally asked quietly.

"Maybe God originally did want me to win a lot of people for Him. But my motives were so selfish, so full of pride. Maybe He asked for the thing I least wanted to give up. In the end I think He wanted me to learn how to be quiet and in the background, enabling others to serve."

Jacie flashed her a beaming smile. Hannah gave her a weak one in return.

"I'm only sorry I didn't get it until the last day."

"At least you got it."

"Sounds like quite the journey," said Joelle.

"It was," Hannah said. "But I'm glad I went through it. I feel humbled. And I hope I never, ever try to do something out of pride again."

"Did you have any more good moments?" Jacie asked, concerned that Hannah had a bad week.

Hannah smiled. "I'd have to say this one rates pretty high." She looked around at the faces of her friends. Phoebe still looked as funky as ever, but now Hannah knew there was more to her than that. Phoebe's words were filled with godly wisdom and strength. Perfect Joelle was no longer a threat. She was a kindred spirit who'd struggled in life and knew redemption. Lia, albeit as crazy now as she was the first day, had proved that being yourself is what really matters—even if people look at you weird. Laurilee, vulnerable and sensitive, had a heart of compassion for others that emerged above the other girls. Even Jacie seemed to be a little more courageous, a little more creative, a little more "Jacie" than she was before. With the exception of Jacie, Hannah hadn't even known these girls' names two weeks ago, and now she couldn't imagine going back to Copper Ridge without them. Here, surrounding her, were girls who loved, accepted, and prayed for her. Girls who had shared wonderful memories with her—from hilarious conversations in the hotel room to hard moments on the mission field.

"Awww. Group hug," squealed Lia. The six girls stood on their towels and crowded into each other, cheek to cheek, until the entire pile collapsed giggling into a cloud of rising sand.

The pale light of dawn barely touched the sky as the girls clumped bleary-eyed down the stairs, suitcases in tow. The teams counted off one more time—Hannah, still half-asleep, had to be jabbed by Joelle before she called out her number.

Team 10 climbed onto the bus for their last trip, this time to the airport. Hannah had barely slept. FUAGNEM went late because everyone wanted the last chance to worship together as a group to last forever. And then the girls spent the rest of their short night packing and talking in their room—sharing tears and their fears about going home. The tears had turned to laughter as the girls shared their most embarrassing moments.

Hannah leaned against the window watching the dim scenery. Jacie leaned comfortably on her shoulder, her breath slow and even.

She had grown so much in the past two weeks that she couldn't believe it. Her heavy eyes drooped. And she smiled to herself. She liked this Hannah better than the one who boarded this bus such a short time ago.

● ● ●

"Hannah, you never told us your most embarrassing moment," Morgan said as some of the Team 10 girls sat cross-legged on the airport floor waiting for the piles of luggage to be checked in.

Ten half-awake girls directed their attention toward Hannah.

"You could take your pick after this trip. Was it the time I performed in front of hundreds of people with a blood stain on the back of my dress? Or was it when I accidentally accepted a marriage proposal with cheese being the only qualification? Or perhaps the day I called one of the most respected men in the entire city of Caracas Dr. Beer?"

The girls laughed. "You've certainly been fun, Hannah," said Joelle.

"I'm really glad ya came on this trip," agreed Laurilee.

"Glad I could keep you entertained," said Hannah.

"Well, that was one of the benefits." Laurilee looked thoughtful.

"But more importantly I've appreciated your convictions and your heart."

Morgan nodded. "I still remember seeing your compassion for that young mom in the hospital. I'll never forget that. It really taught me about loving without being afraid. Your heart for her was so genuine."

"And every time I go to McDonald's, I'll remember how you gave food to that hungry man," said April. "I can still see the look on his face. When I get home, I'm going to keep my eyes open for people like that and do something to help."

Nichole nodded. "One of the first nights when we were talking at dinner, you said you've decided not to date right now—but instead focus completely on knowing God. I thought about that a lot since you mentioned it, and decided I won't date for the next nine months, but instead spend time getting to know Him better."

"Really?" Hannah replied, shocked. "That's great. I don't even remember mentioning that."

"It was really quick. But it sure made an impact on me," explained April.

"I've read the note ya left in my Bible over and over. I'm planning on keeping it there, so I can read it whenever I feel worthless. I think it will be a great reminder of how God sees me," Laurilee half-whispered.

Jacie's dimples appeared alongside her smile. "You're the one who encouraged me to do chalk drawings. If you hadn't been on the team, I probably would have hidden behind the backpacks the whole time."

Lia grabbed Jacie in a side hug. "Yeah, 'cause we'd have never known you were the next Monet. You certainly wouldn't have said anything."

Jacie grinned sheepishly.

Hannah happily allowed the attention to focus on Jacie. For once, it felt good to have praise directed to someone else. Her own face still felt flushed from the unexpected comments of her friends. Joy bubbled up inside.

Thank You, God, that You have Your own plans.

The two weeks in Venezuela had been like nothing she'd imagined. She hadn't preached a sermon and led a hundred people to Christ. But she had clumsily prayed with a sweet little girl. She hadn't been the mentor and Bible teacher for her team, but God had used her to impact their lives in ways she hadn't realized. And God had showed Himself to her in new ways, too.

Jacie took a sharp breath, and Hannah turned to look at her.

"Jared!" she shrieked. "Is that Jared?"

chapter 20

"I don't think so," said Joelle. "Although it does kind of look like him."

Jacie blinked, then followed the man with her eyes until he turned a corner. He had Jared's confident swagger, his jet black hair. Like Jared—but not him. "You're right," she sighed.

Ever since she took the journal from Hannah, she thought she saw Jared everywhere—at the market when they shopped for souvenirs, the mall, the beach, outside the bus windows. More than anything, she wanted Jared to have Marisa's journal. She ached for him. She wanted him to know that Marisa died believing Jared loved her and that she forgave him. *God, please. It would mean the world to him.*

"Did you ever find his address?" asked Joelle.

"No. I don't know his last name, and neither do the trip leaders. They contacted Hank through a local church."

Hannah spoke up. "They told Jacie that if she had come to them earlier, they could have found out. There just wasn't time."

"Can you contact missions organizations when you get home?" Joelle asked, leaning across her backpack.

"What would I say? Excuse me, I'm wondering if you know of anyone named Hank who has a son named Jared who did missions work in Venezuela? There are hundreds of missions organizations in the States. Where would I even begin?"

Joelle groaned. "What are you going to do?"

"I don't know," Jacie said softly. All she could think of was Jared's heartbreak. She could see him staring sadly, vacantly, out the window while the moth beat itself to death. This might soften his grief and help him heal. *God, this has You written all over it. Please help me get Jared and the journal together. Please?*

Joelle and Hannah each gave her a squeeze, then lay down on the airport terminal floor. Hundreds of kids in teal shirts lay on the floor, making it look like a great tragedy had taken place.

A great tragedy has *taken place*, Jacie thought, *that Jared is walking around with this gaping hurt, and he doesn't need to be.*

Jacie took a sweatshirt out of her backpack and bunched it on top of the pack. She lay down and closed her eyes. Images of Marisa floated across her mind. She didn't really know what Marisa looked like. But Jared not only said they looked similar but he had also called her Marisa. Fuzzy images played through her sleepy haze. Marisa, holding hands with Angela. Angela giggling and running from a lumbering bear. Marisa, tears coursing down her face, writing in her journal.

Please, God, Jacie said as her mind drifted into a gray cloud of near-sleep.

"Hey, girls! What a coincidence to run into you at five in the morning!"

That voice . . . Jacie forced her tired eyes open. She looked through the haze to see . . . Hank. It was really Hank. Which meant Jared . . .

She jumped up. "Where's Jared?"

"Well, that's a fine howdy-do," Hank said. "Don't I get a greeting?"

"Hello. But I thought you left already." Maybe Jacie could talk some sense into her dream.

"We spent the last couple days with friends outside of Caracas. I had no idea we'd be at the airport at the same time."

"But where's Jared?" Jacie asked, her heart pumping wildly.

"He went to the restroom. He'll be out in a minute."

"I have something for him."

"Well, okay. You can give it to him." Hank looked a little baffled.

Jacie put her head in her hands, trying desperately to clear her thoughts. *Where is it?* She couldn't think. She grabbed Hannah's shoulders and shook her. "Where's the journal?"

"I don't know, silly. You have it."

Why hadn't she let Hannah keep it? Hannah would've known exactly where she'd packed it. But instead it was somewhere in Jacie's disorganized stuff.

In her suitcase.

She smiled with relief. It was in her suitcase.

Which is in line to get checked!

"I need to find my suitcase," she blurted. She ran to the front of the line where several airline attendants were sorting and putting stickers on over 400 pieces of luggage.

"I'm looking for a blue suitcase. I need it." The attendant shrugged, and Jacie repeated herself more insistently. The attendant held up a finger. "*No hablo inglés.*" He turned and talked with another attendant. *Hurry, hurry,* Jacie thought. She watched as more bags were thrown onto the conveyor belt. *Was that one hers?*

"Yes, Miss?" the second attendant said.

Words flew out of Jacie's mouth. "I need my suitcase. It's blue. My name is Jacie Noland. Have you seen it?" The young man rolled his eyes. It seemed all the suitcases were blue. Many had already been checked. He shrugged his shoulders and went back to his work.

She raced to the huge pile yet to be sorted, digging through it.

"Jacie, what are you doing?" Berk asked.

"I need to find my suitcase."

The other girls joined in the search.

"We're being asked to get to our terminal and load up."

"I just need a few minutes. It has to be here." She rummaged through several piles, tossing aside other suitcases.

"Jacie, we can't miss the flight."

"But I know it's here."

"Jacie, you . . ."

"WAIT!" Jacie was frantic.

Jared came over to them. "You guys need to get going—"

"Found it!" Joelle called, dragging out a worn blue suitcase from the pile.

Jacie tore it open.

"Jacie, we need to go. They just gave the last call."

She flung out articles of clothing. Dirty socks, underwear, shorts, T-shirts . . . the journal.

She handed it to Jared, feeling like she'd nearly explode. "It's Marisa's!"

His eyes widened and he stared at it. "Wow. Where . . . ?" Tears filled his eyes as he turned the pages.

"Jacie, girls, I'm sorry. We need to go now," Berk hastened them.

"Hannah found it when they dug up her house. Read the last page." She was being rushed away in her crowd of friends. "Read it."

That was her last view of Jared. Wet eyes, staring down at a grimy book, holding it like it was a priceless, fragile piece of art. She knew there would be healing when he opened its pages. And she felt weightless at the thought.

● ● ●

Jacie sank into her seat and closed her eyes. Exhaustion pulled at her. But excitement and joy kept sleep at bay. *Oh, God. Thank You. THANK YOU! Thank You for my being sick. Bet You're laughing now, aren't You? All my complaining and whining about being sick, and You used it so I could talk to Jared. Thank You for putting it on Hannah's heart to keep the journal. Thank You for letting us serve You even when we didn't know we were serving.*

"Jell-O Cube!" Gregg's voice filtered through the seatback. "Could I come up and talk to you a minute?"

And I guess there's still more You want to do, God. "Sure, Gregg." She scooted over to the middle seat so Gregg could collapse his lanky body next to her.

He shoved the mop of brown hair out of his eyes but didn't make eye contact. "I wanted," he faded out. "I wanted to tell you I'm sorry."

"For what? I feel like I should be apologizing to you."

"Yeah. You can if you want." He put his goofy face on and pushed it into her space, waiting.

"I'm sorry."

"Okay. Now that you've got that out of the way, I want to say my sorry. Um . . . I guess I thought you liked me because you always smiled at me really big and I thought that meant—"

Jacie thought of Tyler's warning. She'd never tell him he was right.

"Anyway, Corey explained it all to me, and I guess that means you really won't be my girlfriend?" He raised an eyebrow.

Jacie shook her head. She didn't trust what might fall out of her mouth.

"Okay. But can I stay in touch? E-mail? IM?"

She nodded, thinking it best to keep to the silent responses.

"Cool. I'll send you more climbing pictures. Next month, my dad and I are doing Mount Brunswick. It's one of the toughest climbs in Ohio. I need to get conditioned for it beforehand. Start liftin' again and stuff . . ." His voice droned on while Jacie plastered a smile across her face and quickly hid it again. *No, Jacie. Don't smile.*

"Welcome to the Miami International Airport." The nasal voice greeted the friends as they emerged onto the moving walkway, arm in arm.

"Can you believe it?" asked Becca. "We'll be sleeping in our own beds tonight. No cockroaches to smash. Did you ever think we were so incredibly spoiled?"

"I already decided that our townhouse is a palace," Jacie said. "And that I have more clothes than I deserve."

"It changes you, doesn't it?" Tyler asked.

"Is it wrong for me to be glad for what I have?" Jacie asked.

"I hope not," Becca said. "Because I can't wait to lounge by my pool. But as I do, I won't take it for granted anymore."

"What are you glad for?" Tyler asked.

"Taking hot showers in the morning," said Hannah.

"And eating sugar-coated cereal and pancakes and sausage for breakfast," said Jacie. Her stomach rumbled happily at the thought.

"And sleeping in," said Tyler.

"Having a radio with English lyrics on it."

"Brushing my teeth with tap water anytime of the day or night."

"Washing my hands after—well, you know."

"Climbing only one flight of stairs to get to my bedroom."

Yeah, home does sound nice, Jacie thought. She hadn't really been homesick the last couple of weeks, but now that they were getting ready to board the plane to Denver, she was absolutely antsy to see her mom and tell her a hundred stories about the trip.

"Hey," Tyler said, pointing behind Jacie. "Luxury plus."

She turned. The door to a unisex bathroom stood open.

"A bathroom," Hannah said. "So what?"

"Have you forgotten what one looks like?" Jacie said.

"Let's go in." Tyler's eyes lit up.

The three girls eyed each other.

"What are you talking about, Tyler Jennings?" asked Becca.

"C'mon." He ushered the girls inside, and then unrolled many sheets of toilet paper off the roll. He held it up. "Ain't nothin' like a real American bathroom."

"Ohhh, I get it," said Hannah.

"This *is* exciting," added Jacie.

Each of the girls grabbed a huge wad of TP and flung it into the toilet.

"No more throwing gross TP in the trash can!"

"No more fishing it out with a plastic knife!"

"From henceforth and forever we can—"

". . . 1 . . . 2 . . . 3 . . ." they chanted together. "FLUSH!"

"Wow, that felt good," said Tyler.

All four stood staring at the marvel of a toilet that could be flushed.

"Okay, enough already!" Becca said. "We don't want to miss our flight because of a little bit of toilet paper."

The friends spun around and linked arms again.

"So are we coming back next year?" asked Jacie.

The response returned unanimous. "Absolutely!"

"I can't believe we're leaving all our awesome friends."

"We won't get that incredible praise and worship time every night."

"Or Susie's funny talks."

"Or Redman."

"Or really good mangoes."

"Or super-late-night talks."

"Or singing on the bus."

Jacie stuck out her lip. "And no more croutons for breakfast."

All our parents were waiting together outside the security gate for us. It wasn't until later that I realized not one of our parents asked, "How many people did you lead to Christ?" Instead they smothered us with hugs, kisses, and "I missed you so much." In the car, my parents asked, "What do you want to tell us? What are you most excited about? What did God do in your life?" Everything they asked had to do with the changes that must have taken place inside me. All the way home on the plane I had worried they would be disappointed with my lack of evangelism success. It never came up. Not once. They were proud of me. Not for what I did or didn't do, but for who I am and who I have grown to be.

I can't wait to see what God has for me next. I'm going to TRY not to barge in and expect that I know what God will do. I want to be a true bond servant, waiting for instructions from the Master.

● ● ●

The shack smelled so good. The moment I opened the door, my art friends raced out to greet me. The tangy fragrance of oil paints, the warmth of canvas, the pungent aroma of charcoal flooded me. I could only close my eyes and breathe deeply, hoping to let all these become me again.

I shouldn't have worried. I sat, took out a canvas, and expected to paint the stacked homes in Caracas. The tiny chocolate faces of wide-eyed children. The busy, colorful streets filled with cars and people. Instead, I painted myself, standing, staring out across San Francisco bay. Just standing. But leaning. Leaning into the arm wrapped around my shoulder. The arm of my father who stood next to me, looking—not across the bay, but down at me. Even though we were shadows against the setting sun, anyone could see this man admired and loved this girl—his daughter.